Five Old 'GI_
Motorhome

(The Twilight of Our Years)

A novel

by

Michael Rowland

The Five Old 'GITS 'from left to right:

Michael Rowland, Geoff Scott, Mike Riley, Nigel Stephenson, and Steve Wilson.

Five Old '*GITS*' and a Motorhome

(The Twilight of Our Years)

Copyright © 2022

Michael Rowland

All rights reserved.

Photographs of Gibraltar courtesy of Andrew Rowland.

A note to the reader

It's said that Homer once wrote, *'The journey is the thing'.* And the path from idea to a published novel has its own rocky road.

That being said, this novel does have its fair share of ups and downs along the way.

Before I go any further, I would like to point out to you that this book is purely fiction.

During the course of writing this book, I took inspiration from a number of newspaper articles, holiday reviews, and recent media reports, along with several anecdotes and reminiscences from family and friends.

In addition, it's peppered with several true events that happened to me and my family while on holiday in France, plus a touch of poetic licence and a great deal of my imagination. Yet the five old *'GITS'* in question are still alive and kicking.

Acknowledgements

Thank you to my brother, Andrew for the interesting facts about Gibraltar, after living there for a number of years, and for the stunning photographs of Gibraltar.

And a huge thanks to Steve Wilson for his input and support, which makes the story more believable.

*

Additional photographs courtesy of Pixabay.

A Little Nostalgia – courtesy of Margaret Mcintosh.

Get Back – courtesy of Chalkey White.

*

Life is like a camera. Just focus on What's important in your life, and capture the good times ...

Other titles by Michael Rowland

9/11: Official Complicity

9/11: Blank Canvas

Morocco or bust August '69

Praise for the award-winning book, Morocco or bust August '69

"This is a very well-written and thoroughly edited book. It is a joy to read and to remember days past when everything seemed so much simpler.

A group of lads with a rickety, unreliable, untrustworthy van taking off for pastures and worlds unknown has all the elements for a good rollicking tale of adventures abroad! The author masterfully keeps things simple as he recounts the boys' trials and tribulations as they aim for Morocco.. Highly recommended."

Michael is also an award-winning children's author writing under the pen name – Daniel M Warloch (anagram of Michael Rowland).

Children's titles by
Daniel M. Warloch:-

The Leap Year series
Leap Year
Leap in The Dark
Leap of Faith
*

Christmas *Presence*
*

The Jake Hollywood series

The Key to Survival
(Winner of the 2021 TopShelf Indie Book Awards)

We Are Not Alone

Three Shots Rang out In Dallas
*

The Holly KissKiss short stories
Rudolph's Little Helper

A Little Bird Told Me. . .

(Winner of the TCK Children's Short Story Awards 2021)

The Show Must Go On. . .

A Puppy Dog's Tale

A Holly Jolly Holiday

Color My World

Spooktacular

A Heart of Gold

Sticks and Stones

Holly Saves Christmas

Holly's Circus Treat

Stories Paint Perfect Pictures

Are You Sitting Comfortably?

The Little Davey Series

Achieving Your Goal

Living the Dream

Practice Makes Perfect

Overcoming the Odds

* * *

"A man of many talents telling stories for the young, and in the years to come those children will tell their offspring's about Holly KissKiss, and her friends and the adventures they had. All Daniel's books will one day become modern day classics that will stand the test of time."

* * *

"Daniel must have magic in his fingers and pixie dust floating around his head for when he creates a child's story, for only a person who believes in magic could create such wonderful stories in such detail that a child would be mesmerized by listening to them at bedtime, and in doing so enter a beautiful and fascinating world of make believe."

* * *

About the author

Michael Rowland was born in 1949 in the United Kingdom. He found a passion for reading at an early age, yet his desire to write didn't develop until he was in his early sixties.

He lives with his wife of 50+ years, June, in a small village of Oxton, in the Wirral.

Michael has won several awards over the years, including Children's Author of the month in the May 2018 issue of the Wildfire Magazine in the USA, and the TCK Reader's Choice awards 2020, Children's Short Story Award 2021 and the winner of the 2021 TopShelf Indie Book Awards.

Chapter One

There are several amazing places I'll remember all my life—visiting Japan, New York, Berlin, Finland, Sweden, and awesome family holidays in France. But nothing is burnt deeper in my memory bank than the summer of '69 . . .

Fifty-three years ago this year, 1969, six friends and I set off on a holiday of a lifetime to Morocco in a clapped-out van.

One of the seven, Steve Wilson kept a diary, which I adapted into an award winning true story - *Morocco or bust August '69*.

Back then, in what we now know as the swinging sixties, came great music, LSD, hanging around in muddy fields in flimsy tents, and not forgetting, hippy music festivals.

The shackles of what we had become used to had been shed. Young people wanted freedom, and that was the reason we decided back then to go on a holiday with a difference.

The Swinging Sixties was the period between 1964–70 in the UK. These were years of great social and cultural change that made the country what it is today.

By 1969, the sixties were well and truly swinging. It was at its height.

The 1960s in the UK saw the end of capital punishment, divorce reform, abortion, and the legalisation of homosexuality. In the 60s, the campervan played an important role in many people's lives, and you couldn't avoid coming across a psychedelic painted campervan or a converted school bus on the road, or as pictured below, top-of-the-range cars.

John Lennon's Rolls Royce and George Harrison's Mini Cooper

* * *

In the 1950s, VW started production of what was basically a 'box on wheels'. It was a huge success.

VW continued this line of campers up until the 80s.

In the years that followed they gained a cult following and have been the van of choice for generations of hippies, nomads, surfers, festival goers, and rock stars.

In the 1970s some people didn't want the 60s to end so they carried on with the party, putting on big free festivals focusing on music, arts, and culture.

In fact, back in the 60s; one of the seven, Nigel Stephenson, had a Ford Prefect which he'd painted yellow, and adorned with brightly coloured flowers with a Union Jack on the back.

He called it his 'passion wagon', or alternatively, his 'babe magnet'.

Like myself, the others had been successful in their fields of employment, and likewise had children and grandchildren.

We had all made sacrifices and some bad decisions, which was all part of life and growing up.

We all made it in one piece in the end, all of us living full lives.

During the holiday in 1969, Steve met his future wife, Jean. They got married in 1971 before settling down in Scotland; after that we lost contact.

Five of the seven, frequently met over the years, at housewarmings, birthdays, and Christmases, and the topic of conversation was always the holiday in 1969.

With all the milestones and career changes I went through over the years, trying to better myself, moving to different parts of the country, time slowly crept up on me, which resulted in me losing contact with Steve for well over 40 years.

Five years ago, I managed to get in touch with Steve through Facebook.

Back in the 1970s, they was no such thing as social media, but it's still one of my biggest regrets that I didn't get in touch with Steve much earlier.

Since then, five of us try and get together at least once a year.

In fact, it was only a few years ago that we talked about doing it all over again. Like everything else around the world, Covid put a stop to all that.

This year though, 2022, there would only be five of us if we decided to go. One of the seven, Trevor, disappeared off the face of the earth just after we returned from Morocco in 1969, and Pete Armitage bowed out due to health problems. Which left, me, Steve, Geoff, Nigel, and Mike.

I was ten when my family moved from Rotherham to Bradford in 1959. Geoff lived at the top of the road. Steve lived a few streets away. Nigel, Mike, and Pete came onto the scene a few years later.

I went on holiday with Steve and his mum and dad to the Isle of Wight. He says he can't remember. I clearly can.

We boarded a coach in Bradford that took us to London, where we spent a couple of hours before catching the train for the ferry.

I bought an orange, velvet tie in Carnaby Street. If my memory serves me right, it cost me a week's wage.

I think we were 16 or 17 at the time. Steve was a pain in the backside when we got to the I.O.W, insisting that we go onto the pier every sodding night to play bingo, because he fancied the girl who called out the numbers.

According to a recent study, we are a nation of forget-me-nots, failing to remember an average of 1,095 things a year.

A third of us put forgetting phone numbers or where we parked the car down to getting older.

In Steve's case, forgetting this holiday. That's what happened, and I'm sticking to it.

The study did also say that social interaction and exercise boosts the brain power.

When the Covid restrictions were lifted in February 2022 in the UK, we soon organised a trip to Scarborough, staying two nights at the Royal Hotel. Steve came down on the train from Glasgow; Nigel and Mike drove in separate cars; Geoff came on the train from Leeds; and I came on the train from Liverpool. Once again, the topic of conversation was us all reliving the holiday.

Within a couple of hours, we had worked out a cunning plan. Organising another holiday . . . with one slight difference.

We were all married.

We knew we weren't spring chickens anymore; we just wanted to live the dream once again. Who could blame us?

Life advice often consists of people saying you should 'aim for the stars' and plan where you want to be in a year or even five or ten years.

For us five that was completely unrealistic, as we could hardly see beyond the next few years if we were lucky.

That was the reason we wanted to relive the dream while we still could.

Throwing caution to the wind, as they say.

And as luck would have it, Steve had a six-berth, six-seat-belt motorhome.

And more importantly an inside toilet, since as you can no doubt imagine at our age, we would have to stop every hour at a service station.

1969

Front left to right:

Geoff Scott, Michael Rowland, Mike Riley

Back left to right:

Nigel Stephenson, Steve Wilson, Trevor Coates, Pete Armitage

* * *

Oh, to growing old!

Mind you, we weren't tied to a rocking chair with a pipe and slippers with zips and a mug of chocolate, just yet.

We were all retired, so there was nothing to stop us from going. Except . . . getting our wives to let us out of their sight.

Before we met our respective wives, back in the sixties, we used to go to Scarborough most weekends, including one a few weeks prior to us going to Morocco, testing out the van plus the seating arrangements, also the tents.

The campsite in Cayton Bay where we stayed wasn't much to look at. It was little more than a muddy field which sloped downwards at an awkward angle.

On one side of the field there was a few caravans on bricks, permanent fixtures, hopeful that someone, one day, would breathe new life into their damp, musty frames.

In all the time we spent there, not one of us took any notice, which when you looked at the state of them, I wasn't surprised.

As young happy-go-lucky teenagers, we used to spend a great deal of time in The Golden Ball public house in Scarborough, which was a popular haunt for holiday makers, especially those from West Yorkshire.

The pub was situated on the seafront. Opposite it, would you believe, was a blue police phone box, similar to the one Dr Who uses—the Tardis. All of which brings me to what we thought at the time, was a hilarious and, some might say, childish prank while staying in Scarborough one weekend. We came up with a plan to kidnap one of our friends, Pete Wilson, as he was walking on the seafront. Once we had dropped him off at the north end of town, we planned to leave him to walk back while we set off in the van.

The reason we chose Pete was because he was the smallest in the group. As we got close to him, Nigel braked hard, before two of us slid open the side door, both jumping out, then throwing a sleeping bag over Pete's head, then bundling him into the van.

We did it for a laugh, also to see what reaction we would get from the people around. Can you believe it, not one of them reacted, they just carried on walking as though nothing had happened?

Chapter Two

Steve's motorhome has 6 belted seats, a table area that converts to a double bed, a large overhead sleeping area for two people, and a large bed area in the U-shaped lounge at the back. Plus, a satellite TV, cooker, fridge etc.

Back in 1969 there were no such things as seat belts.

My son, Mark, had a two-man tent which I'm sure he would let me borrow. At six foot four, I didn't fancy sleeping on a five foot bed throughout the course of the holiday.

It would also give the others more room to stretch out.

We also agreed that whoever was driving in the morning would have the first choice of using the overhead bed, so at least there was a slim chance of them getting a good night's sleep. However, I would sleep in the tent when we were in Lloret de Mar, having already decided that we would stay there for a few nights on our way home.

And not forgetting the portaloo, which we would take in turns to empty.

The kitchen had a three-burner gas hob with integrated sink, battery-powered fridge with freezer with ample space for keeping food cool.

Finally, before I bore the pants off you, 4x3 points electric sockets, 6xUSB charging points, and an awning, where we could sit at night if it rained.

As far as I was concerned it had all of the bangs and whistles. After two days of reminiscing, we put our plan into action.

We would sit down with our wives, hoping to persuade them to let us go on holiday.

We all agreed that Saturday the 11th of June would be suitable for us all, and we had enough time to organise the trip.

Plus, there was the fact that the Tour de France started on the 1st of July.

The only sticking-point I had was that it was my wife June's birthday on the 12th of June.

I would have to cross that bridge when I got to it. I'm sure if the other wives agreed, she would as well. I hoped so.

I have to admit, at first, Nigel and Mike wanted to drive down in their fancy cars to Morocco, staying in 5-star luxury hotels on the way.

Steve, Geoff, and myself said that if we didn't travel together the whole idea would be called off. After a friendly debate, the two of them agreed that it would make more sense being together, looking after each other, especially being old gits. All we needed now was for our better halves to give us the go ahead.

Chapter Three

Over the next few nervous days, we all waited for the reaction from our wives, by watching our 69ers WhatsApp.

On the third day, we all got the nod, with various conditions, which didn't come as any surprise to us.

We had to text our wives every single day, without fail, and call them every two days, and we had to be on our best behaviour, and not to get into any kind of trouble. Us?

In addition, we had to make sure our *wills* were up-to-date. Charming!

That said, we were more mature and easy going. Just hold that thought for the time being.

June wasn't fussed about us going when it was her birthday, reminding me that at our time of life we tend not to celebrate birthdays. She did stipulate though, that I had to bring her back some cigarettes. I didn't argue.

Geoff was due to have an operation on his knee. It had been cancelled, so Elaine, his wife, insisted we take a wheelchair just in case he was suffering from walking, which at first, he objected to.

After Elaine had badgered him for ten minutes, he begrudgingly agreed to the idea. Elaine said she would hire one for the two weeks.

Nigel's partner, Patricia insisted that he take it easy, due to him having a problem with his blood pressure, plus he was still suffering from Covid, which he had caught while on holiday in Austria in the early part of 2020.

I was on Statins for a short while, due to my high Cholesterol levels, plus I was taking CBD gummies for my arthritis, which seemed to be working. Steve wasn't really suffering from anything serious, and as far as Mike was concerned, well, he never looks any older.

Because it was Steve's motorhome, he was responsible for the service, and insurance for five drivers, including European breakdown cover. We all agreed that we would chip in with the cost, as it was the only right thing to do.

As for me, my excuse to June was that I was putting the holiday down to a mid-life crisis.

She replied by saying: *I think you are well passed that dearest, don't you think? Or maybe recapturing your misspent youth?*

I think she might be right in both cases, but she did admire my enthusiasm. I was left to check out the Covid rules in France, Spain, Gibraltar, and Morocco.

I called into various travel agencies, where I was told if we had two vaccines plus a booster and we had proof, we shouldn't have a problem.

I'd had them all, and I knew they had, as I had already checked.

However, Nigel did mention to me that his doctor had advised him not to have the booster because of his underlying Covid problem, which he said wouldn't be a problem as he had already checked with the NHS, about traveling abroad.

Mind you, he'd been skiing several times over the past six months abroad, without a problem.

As we didn't want to be turned away at any of the borders, I made sure everyone's passport was up-to-date.

As we all know, the first thing you need when leaving the United Kingdom for a holiday abroad, of course, is a passport. Like most people, I have a love-hate relationship with mine. I love its power to whisk me away past a grumpy looking man in a uniform as you hand over your passport, and hate, in my case, the tendency of it going missing when you least expect it, which in my case, is most of the time.

The comedian Michael McIntyre has a very funny routine about the moment you can't find your passport. It's even more funny because practically everyone has had the alarming experience in or on the way to the airport or ferry terminal, repeatedly checking for your passport by patting the pocket, until suddenly you don't feel their assuring bulk.

What follows next is total panic, until you realise that you've been patting the wrong pocket. Then when you realise you haven't lost it, you let out a large sigh of relief, quickly followed by a sharp intake of breath, sucking out all the oxygen within a yard of the other passengers, who in turn are gasping for breath.

Come on, don't deny it. We've all done it at some point in our life.

During the early part of June 2022, there were reports in the press about UK citizens wanting to visit what's called the Schengen zone, which included France and Spain, and having to pay a fee for a European Travel Information and Authorisation

System, or ETIAS for short. That was because the UK wasn't in the EU anymore.

By the time we left, the system hadn't been put into force, thank goodness. More red tape!

Nigel and Mike took on the planning of the route, and Geoff was given the task of putting together a list of basic foodstuffs and essentials, such as coffee, tea, sugar, cereal, and washing up liquid etc.

Each of us were left to take out individual medical insurance. With us all being over 70, it wasn't cheap, I can tell you. In spite of that, we managed to get a good deal by using the same company.

When we were discussing the sleeping arrangements, we decided to take sleeping bags, because blankets would be far too bulky to store.

I'd already decided to take one, as I would be sleeping in the tent most nights.

We would also source a safe for the assortment of medication we would be taking. Plus, any money that needed to be kept hidden. Back in 1969, we took £35, which equates to £520 in today's money.

The only problem having all the money locked away in one place: it would tell any thief exactly where all our money was, so as a precaution, we had several hiding places in the van.

We knew we would have to take much more money this time around, as fuel was costly.

We also had the added cost of the toll roads which we didn't drive on last time, as there were only a few, plus back then we wanted to see some of France, which you tend to miss as you drive around the big cities on the motorways that had sprung up over the years.

A gallon of petrol in 1969 was six shillings and six pence—one shilling and three old pence a litre.

The average price when writing this book was £1.78 a litre which equates to £8.00 a gallon.

At the time of setting off it was just over £6 a gallon in France, so we should be able to save some money.

Averaging 45 miles per hour, we would get 40 miles per gallon.

Bradford to Gibraltar on the quickest route is approximately 1675 miles, which means we would need 42 gallons of petrol at £8 a gallon = £336.00 x 2 = £672 divided by five = £134 each.

In 1969, the world was our oyster, so we had no worries about our health.

With four of us being 73 and Mike at 72, we had to be sensible, and if any one of us fell ill, or we were having problems with the van, we would automatically turn back, at a suitable time.

I personally couldn't wait for the promise of two hot weeks in the sun, sleeping under the stars, driving down to Gibraltar, then onto Morocco, before spending a few relaxing days on the coast in Spain.

I could imagine myself waking up first thing in the morning with the feeling of the damp grass from the early morning dew, under my feet, taking a sip of my first cup of strong coffee, sitting on a chair outside the van, enjoying a few moments to myself, while taking in the early sounds of families waking up around me, all ready for another hot day. Then listening to the other four slowly stirring in the van.

As you can probably guess by now, I'm an early riser.

Chapter Four

Over the following weeks and months, we were in constant touch with each other, ensuring that we were all still up for it, and asking if anyone had had second thoughts. No one had. We were all excited to be going, and trying not to sound too morbid, we all knew in our heart of hearts that it might be the last time we had the chance to be together.

The week before setting off, we had a five way conversation on Zoom, ensuring everyone had done what was asked of them.

After my experience last time, getting badly burnt from laying for hours in the sun without putting on any sun lotion, I had bought enough Factor 50 sunscreen and after-sun to sink a battleship.

I also made sure I had enough ear plugs to last me two weeks as no doubt there would be lots of snoring and farting during the night, especially after having a few beers, or in the other four's cases, a few glasses of whisky. I wasn't a whisky drinker; beer or lager was my favourite tipple.

By the number of bottles, they said they would be taking, they could have opened their own off-licence.

We also agreed that on the way down, we wouldn't drink any alcohol during the day, and only a limited amount in the evening, and if any of us felt that they may have a hangover the following morning, they wouldn't be allowed to drive that day.

The laws in France are very strict, so much so, the police could pull you over and breathalyse the driver, or in some cases, the passenger(s). If you were caught driving under the influence of alcohol, or drugs, they won't have any problem confiscating the vehicle, so to be on the safe side, we took a dozen self-breath testers.

On our last trip, there were only three who had passed their driving tests: Nigel, Mike, and Steve. This time round all of us were competent drivers.

Geoff and myself were used to driving in France as we'd had many enjoyable family holidays over the past thirty years. After weeks of preparing for the trip, the day was suddenly upon us.

Chapter Five

This was it. We were really going, which caused a rush of adrenalin to wash over me. Steve drove the motorhome down from Kilbirnie in Scotland to Bradford on the Friday afternoon, staying overnight at Geoff's house as that was the setting off point.

The rest of us drove over first thing Saturday morning.

Mike and his wife Lynne, drove across from Rochdale; Nigel and Patricia drove over from Steeton; and my wife, June, drove me across the Pennines from Liverpool. This time around, we were setting off during daylight hours.

Apart from our wives and family, some of Geoff's neighbours were gathered outside his house after hearing about five old *gits* going on another intrepid adventure.

My youngest son, Mark, and his fiancé, Caroline, were there to see us off, along with my older sister, Judith, and her partner, Eric, plus a few of Geoff's football mates.

It gave us a real sense of support, and to be honest I was expecting a brass band to make an appearance at some point, or bunting hanging from the trees and houses down the road.

After checking that everything was in order, and most of the money and all the medication was safely locked away in the safe which we kept under the mattress in the overhead bed, including a few other hiding places, we were ready for the off.

Because we were limited to space, basically because there would be five adults living in the van, Steve suggested that we lay out everything on the floor in Geoff's lounge, giving us a better idea of how much of it there actually was.

As we looked at all the stuff in front of us, we questioned if it was worth the space it took up. In fact, we all agreed that what we had in front of us was acceptable.

Medication to last two weeks—checked before they went in the safe.

Money (Euros and UKP)—check.

Passports—check.

Ferry tickets—check.

Insurance papers and breakdown telephone numbers—check.

Clothes—check.

Food—check.

Whisky—check. I know, they love their whisky.

Covid passes—check.

Sat Nav set for Gibraltar—check.

Two spare tyres.

The wheelchair was already safely stored in the van.

To pass the time camping in Spain, I brought along an Amazon Echo with a large assortment of music, especially from the Swinging Sixties, along with a selection of board games just in case we get bored. Unlikely, you say?

At that point we gave Steve £60 for the fuel he'd used to get down to Bradford, and for his return trip home.

Steve ensured us all that he had the necessary items for driving abroad, such as:

Two warning triangles and five reflective vests.

More breathalysers.

Spare bulbs.

Headlamp adapters for driving on the other side of the road.

First aid kit.

GB sticker.

A fire extinguisher, and a fire blanket.

All present and correct, the only thing we needed to do now was to store everything that was laid out on the floor back into the van.

Instead of packing our clothes in suitcases, we agreed to use large black bin bags so we could flatten them when stored under the seats.

We all agreed to take the minimum amount of clothes, knowing that if we ran out of tops and shorts, we could buy some cheap ones in the local markets. Nonetheless, some of the bags still looked as though they were fit to burst, due to the large amount inside.

In addition, we had my two-man tent, a spare camping stove in case of emergencies, a bag of cutlery, tea towels, five pairs of Wellingtons and all-weather, water-proof jackets. And not forgetting a folding table and five folding chairs for sitting outside.

So, with the help of our wives, we all trooped out of the house with our belongings.

Fifteen minutes later, we had loaded up the van.

There was a place for everything and everything in its place, all out of sight. As an afterthought, Steve raised an important point, saying that when we were driving, we had to make sure nothing was left to roll about, or fall on the floor, especially cups and glasses, which when you think of it, made sense.

Teamwork makes the dream work.

Furthermore, we all agreed that at no point during the holiday would we discuss Covid or Partygate, because as far as we were concerned, enough had been said by all.

All the same, please let me leave you with this poem by Brain Bilston's re-worked version of Rudyard Kipling's 'IF', which in my honest opinion totally sums up the vast majority of people's feelings in the UK, about what happened in 10 Downing Street, during lockdown.

If (Downing Street Party Remix)

If you can keep your job when all around you

Lies ravaged from what it is you've done;

If intellect and common sense confound you

And if integrity you have but none;

If you can lie and not be tired of lying,

And pretend you act for the public good,

But then leave the people to their dying

And say you did, sadly, all you could

If you can dream—of nothing more than power;

If you can think—but only of yourself;

If you believe this country's finest hour

Is when the chosen few can gain more wealth;

If you can flout the law with bluff and bluster

And not care whether you are believed,

Or deny with scorn every single blunder

And not care how many you may deceive;

If you can stir up hatred, fear and violence

To create division to suit your ends;

And answer cries for help with silence,

And then laugh about it with your friends;

If you can stretch this country to its limit

Or until it is you've had your fun,

Yours is this land and everything that's in it.

And—as you wished—you'll be PM, my son.

Brian Bilston

I don't think there is any more that can be said on the issue .
. .

That being said, when I was putting pen to paper, the Prime Minister, Boris Johnson, had just resigned as the Conservative leader...

Chapter Six

By 10 a.m. Saturday morning, we said our goodbyes, followed by hugs and kisses from our wives and family.

Just the same, we were all slightly nervous and a little apprehensive.

Hey ho! Life's too short to worry about trivial things.

I have to confess, there was a tear in my eye and a lump in my throat as we disappeared from sight, no doubt leaving our wives to wonder what the hell we'd got ourselves into.

"Let's get this show on the *road*."

Ten minutes later, we made our way across town towards the M62, then the MI down to London, then the M20 to Dover.

As before, we had a kitty for the fuel, which we would top up when necessary.

Steve insisted on keeping hold of it, as he wanted to fill up when required as it was easy for us to put the wrong kind of fuel in, especially in France where there were different types.

Also, he had a better idea of what mileage we could get out of the van, as we couldn't run the risk of running out of fuel, more so in France, where the supermarkets didn't open until noon on Sundays.

This time round, I was going to compile a diary which you are now reading. I hope you enjoy the journey.

In fact, it wasn't your normal diary, it was CAMPERVAN LOGBOOK & JOURNAL which I bought online. We also had a notebook, detailing the medication each of us was on, with the prescribed doses to take each day. That was left to me to keep a close eye on.

Last time we left Bradford we broke down after a mile. Problem with the gears, which was soon rectified with a kick.

This time round, it all went smoothly . . .

We had loads of space to stretch out and we didn't have to sit on each other's laps.

As expected, the journey down the motorway was endless, and not surprisingly boring.

The landscape was dull and monotonous.

There was nothing of particular interest to look out for, apart from offshore, giant wind turbines that whirled silently and furiously as far as the eye could see.

I already knew that, as I'd lost count the number of times I'd driven down this particular motorway.

At one point, I found myself being hypnotised by the white lines and the crash barriers endlessly flashing past ...

The weather was now what they call a drizzle, with low clouds reducing visibility to a few yards.

The temperature in the van had dropped considerably. Steve turned it up a few notches, while we got warm.

Thankfully, the drive down to Dover was uneventful.

We stopped a few times to stretch our legs and aching bones, also to change drivers and to fill up with fuel before we reached Dover.

Being six-foot four, sitting with my legs bent at an awkward angle for hours on end wasn't easy.

We had decided that we would only do four hour driving shifts, so that it would give us time to have a power nap, also to enjoy the journey.

After four hours, we pulled into a service station to get something light to eat, as the ferry wasn't due to set sail until teatime.

Last time we just wanted to get there as soon as humanly possible.

If we hadn't had to drive through small villages and towns last time, we would have missed the architecture and the history of France.

It would be different this time, as we would be travelling most of the way on the motorways.

Two hours later, we had finally arrived at the ferry port, and not unlike any other weekend, there was a slithering snake of vehicles in every shape and form, all creeping slowly towards a man in a high-vis jacket.

Victorian Dover was badly bombed by German bombs and shells between 1940 and 1944, yet there very little evidence of it these days.

Before I knew it, we were being directed onto the bottom deck of the ferry. We all piled out of the van, then straight up the metal stairs to the upper decks that played host to your typical duty-free shops, bars, lounges, and restaurants.

The five of us went up to the outer deck to watch as we left the port, taking in the smell of salt and diesel oil, the deep roar of the ship's engines vibrating through the soles of our feet.

Minutes later we stood watching as England disappeared into the horizon, the wind fingering through what little hair we had, before the last sliver of land slipped into an endless expanse of blue, then turning our attention to more pressing matters. Like breakfast.

An English breakfast, knowing full well that it would be hours before we got another decent, hot meal. The noisy restaurant was made up of dozens of people of every shape, size, colour, creed, and nationality.

There were families over three generations who all seemed to be talking at once; well-groomed young couples clearly taking their first joint holiday abroad; young men with salon tans and highlighted hair, pouting and posing to their heart's content; scruffy-looking students types flirting with each other in a prelude to holiday foreplay; and us five relatively well-dressed, seventy-something men suffering from varying degrees of hair loss and old-age ailments.

Back in 1969, six out of the seven smoked. Nearly everyone did, back in those days. Yet over the years we all gave it up.

That didn't stop us wandering around Duty Free, especially myself, as I wanted a case of beers.

I might have a tipple of whisky during the trip. But you cannot beat a cold beer.

While heading across the English Channel Nigel pulled out a folded paper map showing us which route, we were taking.

This was to make sure none of us wanted to stop at any particular place on the holiday.

We all said we weren't all that bothered, which was fine by me, as I'd stopped at plenty of places of interest in France over the years. Plus, we had the added bonus of having a state-of-the-art Sat Nav fitted in the van, as we didn't want to spend most of our holiday wrestling with a 1:1 scale foldable map, the size of a baby's blanket.

As far as I could work out, after leaving Calais, we would then bypass Rouen, Le Mans, Bordeaux, Toulouse, Valencia, Segovia, Merida in Spain, Seville then Gibraltar.

As I'd mentioned before, we had already agreed weeks ago that we would spend a few days in Lloret on the return journey, hoping it may bring back a few memories, especially for Steve. Satisfied with the route, we then rang our wives to let them know that we had arrived safely in Dover, and we were now on our way across the English Channel.

All of us were told once again to be on our best behaviour, and to keep taking our pills.

I mentioned to the others my brother Andrew, who used to live in Gibraltar, and who visited it at least once a year, telling me that you could no longer go by boat from Gibraltar to Morocco as they had stopped it four years ago.

The only other means, apart from flying that is, was to catch a ferry in Algeciras in Spain.

We said we would decide what to do when we got to Gibraltar.

On our last trip, we had a major problem getting into Gibraltar, which was down to Francisco Franco, who had ordered the closing of the borders between Spain and Gibraltar.

(Francisco Franco Bahamonde was a Spanish general who led the nationalist forces in overthrowing the Second Spanish Republic during the Spanish Civil War and thereafter ruled over Spain from 1939 to 1975 as a dictator, assuming the title Caudillo).

To be honest, this trip was kind of déjà vu. In addition to the Franco problem, in 1969 the local newspaper, the T&A, ran a small article about our trip along with a picture.

This year, after Geoff had been in touch with the editor of the paper, another small article was published.

We refused to have our picture taken this time.

The ferry crossed the Channel on a rough, churning sea. It felt like force ten to me. Steve assured us all it was only a moderate swell, not even a proper gale.

I was hoping for calmer waters because I could feel my breakfast churning in my stomach.

I'm not one of nature's travellers, though; in fact, on one of our return family trips from France a few years ago, the sea was so bad it took the helmsman/pilot of the ferry at least four tries to dock in Dover.

Steve was used to ferry crossings, especially when delivering barrels of whisky, and popping over the islands of Scotland in the motorhome for a holiday.

Chapter Seven

As the ferry pulled into Calais, the western horizon glowed a deep sapphire, the rich blue fading as the sun dragged itself deeper beneath the sea, before a tannoy announcement boomed out telling the passengers we were allowed to return to our vehicles.

Because we knew we were nearing Calais, we had already made our minds up to head over towards the stairway that led down to the deck where we were parked.

As we arrived, it looked as though everyone else had the same idea.

Once the ferry had docked, one of the staff slid open the metal concertina gate. We then followed the long line of passengers, winding our way down through the boat to the car deck.

Because of the narrow stairways, there was a traffic jam of sweaty bodies waiting to squeeze themselves into the stairwell.

We weren't having any of it. Steve and Nigel stood shoulder to shoulder in front of us, while Mike, Geoff and myself slowed down to give the ones below time to get onto the deck. When you reach our time in life you don't give a damn about other people.

We weren't prepared to put up with other people's bad manners and nonsense, so we made sure none of them got past us.

The ferry, which was still slowly reversing into port, was heaving, then starting with strong tremors, sending deep, resonating judders that rattled by bones, before docking with a gut-churning grumble.

Following five minutes of pushing, shoving and elbows in ribs, we eventually found ourselves by the van. Fifteen minutes later, we were driving over the ship's ramp and onto French soil.

At that point Steve called out something about it being the first leg proper.

The rest of us agreed with him, remembering the last time we'd left Britain, hitting France, then heading south . . .

It was slightly overcast, not raining, the skies a feathered grey, the road dead straight; fields unrolled left and right, very flat, just the odd tree here and there to interrupt the horizon.

I was feeling a little apprehensive and a little excited. I didn't let it show. I was now thinking, *What the hell am I doing?*

I kept the thought to myself, deciding to take each day one at a time. During the Second World War, most of Calais had been razed to the ground. Now it was a thriving port.

Over the years, the French had built mile after mile of motorways, which linked to all of the major towns and cities in France, which would make our journey much quicker and safer.

Back in 1969, we had no alternative but to drive on the D roads, which took you through small villages and took ages, due to the number of traffic lights and reduced speed limits and endless roundabouts.

I can remember when we went on family holidays when our two sons were younger, you could see motorways being built in the distance, only to be driving on them the following year and spotting yet another motorway being built.

Unlike the British government, the French government looked after drivers. Plus, you had the added bonus in France of hundreds of first-class rest areas and service stations, where you can park a motorhome overnight at no cost.

Unlike in 1969, we didn't have to drive through the centre of Calais, because there was now a motorway that took you around the town, towards Rouen.

Once the ferry had docked, we all imagined the other caravans, campervans and motorhomes would head off into Calais, before setting up camp for the night, spending the evening eating *moules* and *frites* in some fancy beach bistro. It didn't work like that.

The motorway going south was a convoy of caravans, motorhomes, campervans etc. etc. . . . .

That didn't bother us in the slightest as we weren't in any rush.

They say the road of friendship never runs smooth. In our case, it couldn't have been further from the truth.

I've known these four guys for well over sixty years and I can honestly say that I can't remember us falling out.

Sure, we had a spat or three. But we soon made up, as we knew life was too short to bear grudges.

Chapter Eight

During the first hour of the drive, we talked about what we'd expect this time round, when we called into Lloret de Mar.

A couple of us had visited it since 1969, including me. That was a long time ago, yet for the life of me I couldn't remember much of it.

The road was getting busy, and despite their good intentions, the huge articulated vehicles that are a universal feature on most motorways all over the world, couldn't help but scare the crap out of us when they passed.

First came the huge bow-wave of air they displayed, shoving us forcibly towards the gravelly verge, before a vacuum suck of slipstream pulled the van violently back towards the centre of the road.

The whole experience was horrible, but in this case, Steve was driving, which helped a great deal since, as I said before, he delivers barrels of whisky all over Scotland in what I can only describe as a big bloody lorry.

Now this is when it gets a little spooky.

As I was slowly drifting off to sleep from the rhythm of the van, I thought my eyes were playing tricks with me.

In my mind's eye, I could clearly see the seven of us in the Bedford van back in 1969, as though I'd stepped into another dimension, some kind of time warp. The smell of diesel fumes, cigarette smoke, all five of us squeezed together like sardines on the bench seat.

I dozed off with that wonderful thought in my twenty-year old mind. I was so tired I could have slept on a washing line.

I'd only been asleep for what felt like a few minutes, before we pulled into what the French call an 'aire de service' or as we know them, a service station.

These are not your typical UK service stations. No, these are so much better.

I wasn't sure where we were until I spotted the large green frog by the side of a lake. Clearly the French do have a sense of humour.

When taking family holidays in France, we always made a special effort to stop at this particular service station for a rest.

In the 60s and even the 70s, the service stations in the UK were uniformly dismal places, serving what they called food that tasted of nothing if you were lucky, or like eating the bottom of a bird's cage if you weren't.

Meanwhile, the temperature had dropped a few degrees as the wind grew stronger.

As in the UK, there are a number of approved parking bays for motorhomes and campervans.

Most of them have disposal points, where you can pay a couple of pounds to empty your waste tank and toilet, then refill with fresh water.

This was also the case in France.

More importantly, you are allowed to stay overnight at no cost. The only drawback, if you are really exhausted, is that lorries will come and go at all hours, so we made sure our parking spot was well away from them, in a designated area.

They also provide fuel, clean toilets, a shop etc.

Also, according to French traffic law, you may park at the side of the road, but when stepping out, always watch out for traffic.

By this time, I was dog-tired and hungry, desperate for bed, but underneath it, thrilled to bits to be on holiday with my mates.

After freshening up, we called into the shop for something basic to eat, such as a sandwich, crisps, and a bottle of water.

By 10 o'clock that night, we were tired, and it was well past our bedtime, so we decided not to travel through the night, and carry on in the morning, also we had parked in a decent spot.

What followed next with Mike was something I'll remember for years to come.

He decided he wanted to sleep in the overhead bed, which was a challenge in itself.

As he was attempting to climb up, the rest of us sat back watching him, while passing a pleasant ten minutes while Mike struggled to the summit, which mostly involved grunts, swimming legs, and invitations for the rest of us to go forth and multiply.

His posture at this point brought to mind a shipwreck victim clinging to a piece of floating wreckage on rough seas, while holding on for dear life to the side of the frame, his right leg trying to reach up over the mattress.

By this time, my cheeks were aching from laughing so much.

We couldn't watch him struggle any longer, so Steve and myself gave him a helping hand.

It was then when Steve pointed out to Mike, that there was a ladder he could have used, resulting in the air turning blue again.

His face flushed, he looked down on the four of us before pointing out that he'd use one of the other beds next time.

Moments later, we were all flaked out.

I relaxed on one of the benches, stretching out my long legs, while the others made themselves comfortable where they were sat.

Chapter Nine

We'd only been settled down for a few minutes when there came a noise outside, followed by someone banging on the window in the side door of the van.

Steve was nearest.

I looked up as he pulled the curtain to one side, before Steve whispered over to us that there was an odd-looking guy loitering outside.

He didn't open the door at first, so I got up and stood behind him, as he opened the door.

I made a comment, something like "I've got your back, Jack", causing us all to fall around laughing.

The guy just wanted some milk.

Once Steve handed over what was left of the milk, he locked the door, before we all settled down for the night, my heart beating ten to the dozen.

Steve took a deep breath, before enlightening us about camping in a motorhome. He started off by saying that it can be a tense moment when a stranger knocks on the door. You have to make a snap decision whether to open it or not, because all you have to base your decision on is what that person looks like. You have to listen to your gut.

Anyhow, at least in this case, it wasn't an escaped axe murderer on the loose. If you have read the Morocco book you will know what I am on about.

Ten minutes later, all I could hear was snoring, farting and the wind that had suddenly sprung up, rocking the van.

I slowly fell asleep, imagining myself wandering around the campsite in Lloret, in the cool evening air, with my logbook tucked safely in my shorts pocket, and my trusty pen behind my ear, before giving myself the peace and tranquillity to sit down and put pen to paper of the adventures we had done so far ...

Thanks to our long day, none of us stirred until mid-morning. When we eventually woke up, it took us another half hour to get the kinks out of our weary bones, and for me to hand out the pills. Hey, come on, just you wait until you are well into your 70s. Because of Nigel's problem with his blood pressure, the first thing he did was pull out his blood pressure monitor from his backpack.

While he was checking it, he said that normally blood pressure starts to rise a few hours before you wake up, then continues to rise during the day, peaking in midday.

Blood pressure normally drops in the late afternoon and evening. Blood pressure is normally lower at night while you're sleeping.

His blood pressure was fine. Before you ask, over the holiday, his blood pressure was stable.

Must have been the company he was keeping.

Once we were all back in the land of the living, we headed towards the main building to freshen up.

We could have done it in the van, but with five of us, we would have got in each other's way, plus we could use the showers, before grabbing a bite to eat, as we didn't want to mess about making some breakfast in the van.

We wanted to get on the road as soon as possible.

After each of us had a refreshing shower and changed into something more suitable for the warm weather ahead, we sat in the small eating area. Can you believe it, I was the only one in long trousers!

While the others were texting their wives, I called June, wishing her a happy birthday. I pressed the speaker function on my phone, so that the five of us could sing a pathetic rendition of Happy Birthday to her. Out of tune and out of sync

Even the ones in the cafeteria joined in – mostly in French. But everybody knows the song.

She forgave me again for going on the trip, reminding me not to come back without her cigarettes.

She also thanked me for the birthday card that I'd left on the coffee table, which I'd secretly hid under her iPad.

After saying goodbye, promising June that I'd keep in touch, I spent a few minutes reading the messages from family and friends, all wishing us a good luck, before heading back to the van.

I hadn't realised how relaxing it would be, travelling in a motorhome, which on the face of it, is a bit like camping, with a few mod cons. I can well imagine anyone having a motorhome or campervan being able to access all sorts of beautiful places whilst living close to nature and having no ties to one location.

It's most definitely more comfortable than camping, recalling the trip in 1969.

This time, we had everything with us: books, music, gas, and electricity, and we can be warm and dry and have proper cooked meals. Everything we needed was at our fingertips.

Plus, we had the comfort of a small house. The world was our garden.

By the time we had finished our meal, the sun was out in force.

What's the holiday saying? 'Sun's out, Short's on'.

As you may gather from the photograph at the start of the book, I tend not to wear shorts; only on holidays abroad.

Knowing that the others wore them all year round, even in the winter, I decided prior to the holiday to spend a few weeks sat, relaxing in the garden in my shorts as I didn't want my legs looking pasty. After I'd changed into my new, posh, Chino shorts, I can honestly say to my relief that my legs were as tanned as the others.

Along with my shorts, I had my Genesis, *Last Domino* T-shirt and sandals, minus socks.

Because the guys weren't used to seeing me in shorts, I was expecting a few comments. To my surprise, nothing was said. In fact, Geoff pointed out that we were wearing the same brand of shorts.

On the odd occasion, when the sun was unbearably hot, I took off my shirt. Not for long though, as I tended to get sunburnt, plus I didn't want to upset the neighbours if they were eating outside.

Also, when I removed my T-shirt on the beach, I didn't want to discover that my body resembled a large sack of mashed potato.

Chapter Ten

After breakfast, and taking our medication, making sure everything was secure in the van, we agreed that we would stop shortly after lunch for a substantial, hot meal.

Wait for it. MacDonald's, would you believe, knowing that the French MacDonald's had a great choice of flavours in their McFlurry's range.

If Pete Armitage had been with us, he'd be in his element, working out the mileage between stops, calculating petrol costs, how much we'd spent so far, all down to the last euro.

Making sure we had disposed of all the waste, we drove back onto the motorway, the temperature rising steadily as the morning wore on.

While Nigel was driving, Bryan Adams was informing us on the radio that *'Jody got married'* in the Summer of '69.

We were making good time, and we were soon passing Rouen.

(Rouen, capital of the northern French region of Normandy, is a port city on the river Seine.

Important in the Roman era and Middle Ages, it has Gothic churches, such as Saint-Maclou and Saint-Ouen, and a cobblestoned pedestrian centre with medieval half-timbered houses.

The skyline is dominated by the spires of Cathédrale Notre-Dame de Rouen, *much-painted by Impressionist Claude Monet).*

Already it was turning into a glorious summer's day, the sky a deep blue, the fields sun-kissed with yellow sun flowers on either side of the road.

The sun was properly up now, starbursting on the windscreen, making me squint even with my sunglasses on.

Traffic shot past, gleaming bonnets catching the sun.

We opened the windows and were greeted by the warm, still air, heavy with the scent of sage and lavender.

I went back to staring out of the window at the lush green vineyards rolling past, dark grapes ripening in the summer heat.

Off in the distance, the conical black tower of an ancient chateau stood out against the skyline.

By the time we had reached the outskirts of Le Mans at lunchtime, there wasn't a cloud in the sky.

We were getting hungry, so we decided we would stop at the next McDonalds for a Big Mac and fries, and a McFlurry's.

After a few miles, we drove past a large billboard advertising a McDonalds five kilometres away.

Now wait for it, because here comes the edge-of-the-seat scenario.

Mike was driving. Last time we were together in France, he asked us all for directions.

Someone said over the next roundabout.

And yes, you've guessed it. He drove straight across . . .

When we were a few metres from the turn off, I can't remember who it was, they instructed Mike to turn right here.

He did as he was told.

He turned the wheel over to the right, losing control of the van for a moment, throwing us off balance.

Regaining control, the van careered up the kerb at speed, and up a slight incline, the sudden jolt enough to make us jump out of our seats.

The van then ploughed its way through a line of bushes, with a gap that was just about wide enough for the van to pass through, chopping off leaves and branches in the process then finding ourselves on a grass verge on the other side that ran around the car park.

For a split second, the van went airborne at the top of the crest, sending the van crashing down on two wheels, before it bottomed out.

The van began to shudder violently over the grass, the sound of grunting and cursing in the background, along with rattling crockery, bottles, and God knows what else that wasn't nailed down.

By this time, the five of us were bouncing up and down in our seats.

Steering the van down a small decline, bumping over the concrete edge bordering the car park, Mike finally slowed down, before pulling up by a parking spot close to the entrance. I was hoping the van had taken all of the abuse that had been thrown at it.

As you can imagine we just sat there, dumbfounded, speechless for what felt like hours, but was only minutes.

I don't know about the others, but I breathed in rapid, shallow inhales and exhales, trying to control my frayed nerves.

Instead of getting out of the van to check the undercarriage, the other four unbuckled their seat belts, and dashed to the back of the van.

They were inspecting the bottles of whisky, hoping that the bumpy ride hadn't caused any of them to be broken.

From where I was sat, I heard a huge sigh of relief.

Satisfied none of the bottles were broken, we then decided to check out any damage to the van.

I knew my bottles of beer were safe as I had wrapped two of my beach towels around them, stopping them from rattling.

After a close inspection, the van looked as though there was no obvious damage.

It was only after stepping inside McDonald's, ordering our food, and sitting down at the table, that we all burst out laughing. It was at least five minutes before Steve gave Mike a rollocking.

Putting on his best hurt impression, Mike apologised, adding to his defence that he'd heard someone say next right, which he'd followed to the letter.

There was a brief further exchange between Steve and Mike before they shook hands.

Once the laughter had died down, and after finishing our meal, we went to the toilets to freshen up, before setting off again, Mike insisting he would carry on, as he'd only been driving for an hour.

Pulling out of the car park, he drove on the left hand side of the main road, round a roundabout the wrong way, with Steve shouting out for him to pull over to the right when it was safe to do so, saying that he would take over.

In all the years we'd been friends, growing up in our teens, there had rarely been any falling out between us.

All things considered, and in *Steve's* defence, he had every right to lose his temper. It was his motorhome.

(The 24 Hours of Le Mans is an endurance-focused sport car race held annually near the town of Le Mans, France. It is the world's oldest active endurance racing event).

Le Mans was mainly a market town for the agricultural products of the region until the mid-19th century, when new industries developed and later expanded, principally producing railway, motorcar, and agricultural machinery; textiles; and tobacco. Over time certain of these activities have been reinforced, notably the vehicle and related components industries and food processing. More recently, the plastics and electronics industries have been added, as well as a growing service sector, especially the insurance industry and a university.

Chapter Eleven

It was just after 9 o'clock on Sunday evening by the time we reached Toulouse, after stopping for a cup of coffee at one of the service stations on the way, and to stretch our legs.

(Toulouse, capital of France's southern Occitanie region, is bisected by the Garonne River and sits near the Spanish Border.

It's known as La Ville Rose ('The Pink City') due to the terra-cotta bricks used in many of its buildings. Its 17th-centuary Canal du Midi links the Garonne to the Mediterranean Sea, and can be travelled by boat, bike or if you prefer on foot).

The sun was marginally less intense than it had been all day, but you could just about fry an egg on the pavement.

By this time, we couldn't be bothered looking for somewhere to eat, so we pulled into a picnic area, deciding we would use the facilities in the motorhome. Once we had found a quiet spot well away from the main road and the line of heavy vehicles in the lorry park, we made a start on a spaghetti bolognaise, plus slicing a couple of crispy baguette we'd purchased at the last stop, along with a few cream cakes to finish the whole meal off.

We also made sure we wouldn't get blocked in.

For the moment, the area wasn't full, aware that it may fill up by the morning.

The last thing we needed was to get blocked in, then have to knock on a few cab doors . . .

We all loved the feeling of being able to pull up to a beautiful spot, with a view that's not even possible in a hotel, with most of everything in the van. It was while preparing the meal, I noticed from looking at the other people in the rest area that it was mostly older people who drove this kind of large motorhome.

Maybe this is the kind of thing to get if you've just retired and you want something comfortable, with all the facilities of a house—and by that time in life have enough savings to spend.

Why not, I asked myself. Good for them.

I did notice during the holiday that the bigger the vehicle the more difficult it was to navigate around big cities and towns and also manoeuvre.

I pointed out those facts to Steve, who in turn said that he'd taken into account the sizes of motorhomes, plus the fuel consumption when he'd bought this one.

After working out where we were, we reckoned that the border was at least another 3 hours away, before crossing the Pyrenees, plus another 6 hours to Valencia, then another 8 hours to Gibraltar.

With that in mind, we decided after the meal, we should stay put, as it was a great place.

Also, we didn't want to drive up and down the mountains in the dark.

We took it in turns making the meal. Steve did most of it, as he was used to the hob, while the rest of us set up the fold-out table outside, hoping we wouldn't be inundated with midges.

To our joy, they left us alone so we could eat in peace.

As we agreed, only a little alcohol was consumed, as we couldn't afford to be stopped by the police, ruining our holiday.

Would you believe it, Steve even had a copy of *The Camper Van Cookbook,* which came in handy?

After the meal we washed the dishes, threw away the rubbish, then called our better halves, giving them the good news, that we were still in one piece, adding that we hadn't had any fall outs or any breakdowns, or frightening encounters (apart from Mike's encounter. We kept that between ourselves).

I know I'm repeating myself, thinking back over the last 60 plus years, knowing these four friends, I cannot remember arguing. In fact, I would trust all of them with my life.

I know I am a big softy at heart, and over the last five years I had become more emotional, which meant every mile that took me away from home, further away from my family, and increasingly I felt the loneliness of not being with June ...

Chapter Twelve

The sun was shining the following morning. Three days in a row now. That, in British terms, constituted a summer as far as I was concerned.

I was on the rota to drive next, but only until we reached the start of the Pyrenees, as Steve felt he should be the one driving across the mountains, which I have to admit, was fine with me.

I wasn't worried as I have driven dozens of times in France. In fact, I found it easy driving on the right hand side of the road.

All I wanted was a few minutes to get to know the gears plus any quirks.

After familiarising myself with the vehicle, we set off at a steady pace. It was 9 o'clock in the morning when we left Toulouse, so by my reckoning, we should arrive at Perpignan by lunch time and Valencia by 6 o'clock in the afternoon, where we had already decided to stay the night so we would arrive refreshed in Gibraltar the next day.

After an hour we could see that the traffic was building up. A few minutes later we knew why. There was a diversion.

Why is sitting in traffic so much worse than driving? I would rather drive for eight hours than sit in traffic for four. At least if you are going at sixty, there's some sense of progress.

We weren't stood for too long, before I followed the slow-moving traffic onto the slip road, then finding ourselves driving through the countryside, which we were pleased, as by this time we'd had enough of the motorway.

As the roads got narrower and the villages smaller, we had to slow down, due to the build-up of traffic, including several traffic lights. And, not surprisingly, hordes of picnicking families relaxing by the side of the road. I can't imagine how much dust gets into their food.

Passing through every tiny hamlet, it seemed they imagined it wouldn't be taken seriously without at least one mini roundabout, and dozens of window boxes crammed full of beautiful flowers, and streetlamps all dressed in hanging baskets.

By this time, three of us needed to go to the toilet, so we pulled up in one of the villages.

From the outside the toilet looked fine, yet the inside was a sight for sore eyes. The stench coming from it, was causing my eyes to water.

It was what we called the dreaded 'bomb bog'. It was just a hole cut out in the middle of the floor, with two markers to place your feet.

A roll of toilet paper sat to the right of the hole and to the left was a pile of French newspapers and magazines on an old wooden table that had seen better days.

Years of neglect had taken their toll: there were no discernible signs of upkeep. In fact, by the looks of it, we may have used it in 1969.

Damp was creeping up the walls, the darkness almost like a living entity. I shivered at the sight, and the smell.

Steve waited outside, stopping anyone from disturbing me.

We had no choice but to use the toilet, trying to hold our noses while spending a penny. Beggars can't be choosers.

We were soon on the move again.

After five miles or so, the Sat Nav directed us off the main road and up through one tiny hamlet after another, sleepy villages of narrow streets and ancient stone walls and crooked houses that looked as though a strong wind would knock them down, while old men sat impassively in the shade watching us pass by.

We peeled off onto an even smaller road that climbed higher, winding back and forth up a hill where vineyards gave way to dark pine trees, finally emerging onto the crest of a hill.

The villages and hamlets can only be described as peasants-and-poppies rurality, which was an astonishing contrast to the major towns and cities in France.

We were passing through another village now, and between the houses the view was breath-taking.

Distant hazy blue hills lay behind tumbling fields of sunflowers and grapevines.

I could just make out dark turrets from a number of Chateaus in the distance.

There was something mythical about the place. As though it was some kind of film set, where swashbuckling movies were made.

Ten minutes later, of course, we were lost. The diversion signs had vanished.

Fortunately, I could see the motorway in the far distance, so I just headed in that direction.

Away from the roundabouts and the traffic lights, out across the fields, we soon found ourselves back on the motorway.

We were in three lanes of motorway now with the massive sprawl of the city looming over to our right.

Next, we would have to drive over the Pyrenees. Nevertheless, I wasn't looking forward to it one little bit ...

Chapter Thirteen

After changing drivers, we left the outskirts of the city, the quality of the road much better than the last time we were here, though some of the bends were horrific; one mistake on a corner at speed and it would be the last corner we got wrong.

Steve was taking it easy, even though we had a small convoy of cars and trucks following us.

I did notice, to my relief that the roads had improved tenfold since being here the last time, which on the face of it didn't surprise me.

Many of the roads through the Pyrenees were pretty narrow, but in fairly good condition.

We didn't have much trouble, even on the roads that were one lane wide in some sections. We only had to back up for another vehicle once.

But we did have a bit of a white-knuckle moment when a big truck decided not to wait for us to back up to a turnout on a road that was about 1-1/2 lanes wide.

But other than that, it was fairly stress free.

What makes the Pyrenees so attractive as a driving environment is that the lanes sit on the very bedrock of the two countries, many of them lying on the oldest rocks in Europe dating back 530 million years.

A small part of the roads we were driving on had been worn down by carts and vehicles over thousands of years.

Steve required a high level of concentration, as a misjudged approach could see us taking home the impression of a dry-stone wall on the bodywork.

As he reached each hairpin turn, he slowed the van to a crawl, before gently accelerating through the curves, as gingerly as driving on ice.

The road seemed to be bolted onto the mountain, rock walls chiselled in great slabs at an angle, giving me the feeling, they were pressing in on me.

Even the leaden sky and dull landscape became a region of mystery and enchantment.

The climb into the twisty stuff was invigorating; a beautiful vista stretching out before us.

As we got higher, the clouds swept in low and dull, and it was suddenly misty.

By the time we reached the high ground, we were completely in the clouds, in an eerie stillness, where cars appeared from a fluffy horizon less than twenty metres away, then disappeared just as fast into a wall of cloud behind us.

On the radio, the Beatles were telling us that we were on 'The long and winding road that leads to your door', or in our particular case, hopefully, Morocco . . .

The roads by now were smooth. I was really enjoying myself, thinking it would be nice if it was like this all the way . . .

The scenery was stunning, breath-taking: mountains banked with heather and massive stands of trees, far too many to count, and lines of which had been cut back. It made me feel as though it had no overbearing worries about the miles, we were going to drive over the next two weeks.

It didn't take long for us to cross over the Pyrenees.

Be that as it may, there were plenty of hairy moments.

Eventually we reached the border between France and Spain.

As it was back in 1969, we passed through without a problem.

Already the country had a different feel to it: the gentle rise of the hills, the shadow of pine trees on the horizon.

Chapter Fourteen

Valencia was at least another five-to-six-hour drive, so we drove for an hour before pulling into an *'aire de repos'*, which just had a picnic area and a toilet, so we could stop for a rest for a while and a bite to eat.

Just as we were settling down, we once again got disturbed by someone knocking on the door. Steve told whoever it was outside to bugger off, or words to that effect.

It was the police. They wanted us to open the door.

Shit!

Steve opened the door, before apologising to the two officers who, would you believe, were leaning on the van, smoking.

They said that they'd had a report that there was a great deal of noise coming from our van.

At this point, Nigel took over, pointing out to the officers that all we wanted to do is get some well-earned rest, as we have been on the road for hours.

One of the officer stood on the threshold of the van, peering inside. Once he'd realised, we were just five harmless old men on holiday, they left us alone.

It took us all of one minute to realise the best thing to do was to drive off.

Geoff got into the driver's seat, before setting off.

Moments later, the police car overtook us with their blue lights on. A bit over the top, I thought at the time.

Maybe they were genuinely looking out for our safety.

According to the Sat Nav, after stopping in Valencia for the night, we would have another 8 hours driving before we reached Gibraltar.

That didn't concern us, as we were enjoying each other's company, plus the added experience of driving a home on wheels.

We were making good time, reaching Valencia in the afternoon, due to the roads being quiet.

All we needed now was somewhere to park for the night. That was when my Camperstop Europe guide came in useful.

I bought it a number of years ago, when June and I were thinking of buying a campervan, which was great on paper. In the end, we decided not to bother.

In spite of that, it now looks as though it was the right decision, especially with the high cost of fuel at the moment.

The van would have been rusting away on the drive or in secure storage.

Even so, the guide may have been out-of-date, but it was useful.

When putting the holiday together, I checked out the various camp sites in Valencia, listed in the book, which had pitches for motorhomes.

With the help of the Sat Nav, we easily made our way to Camping Coll Vert, which was only a few miles away from the motorway.

I had phoned the site weeks ahead of us going, asking them if I could book a pitch.

Ten frustrated minutes later, trying to understand what the lady on the other end was saying in broken English, I somehow managed to book a pitch for £13.29. Odd number, I thought at the time.

I knew she'd taken the booking because she had taken the money out of my account, then sent me the confirmation by email.

(The port city of Valencia lies on Spain's south-eastern coast, where the Turia River meets the Mediterranean Sea.

It's known for its City of Arts and Sciences, with futuristic structures including a planetarium, and oceanarium and an interactive museum.

Valencia also has several beaches, including some within nearby Albufera Park, a wetlands reserve with a lake and walking trails).

Driving towards the reception, we passed a pizza place close to the entrance, and by the lights on inside, looking as though it was still open for business.

We pulled up to let Nigel and Mike get out, so that they could order a few pizzas before they closed, while we carried on driving to the reception to make them aware we had arrived.

After filling in the necessary forms and being shown where our pitch was on the map of the site, Nigel and Mike were just coming out of the pizza place, carrying three boxes apiece, looking as though they were carrying two dozen eggs.

You could smell the cheese and garlic from ten yards.

As the evening wore on, the light was beginning to fade when we reached our pitch, the night chorus of birds, combined with the rustling in the undergrowth.

That being the case, we brought out the small table and five folding chairs, before tucking into the pizzas.

Boy they were tasty.

We then spent the next couple of hours reminiscing about our lives and what we'd done.

Because Steve had been out of the picture for a number of decades, he just sat back, listening, taking it all in.

I couldn't help sense by looking at Steve's face that he would have liked to have been involved in just a small part of our lives.

Before we settled down for the night, we texted our wives, informing them that we were all still in one piece.

Because we were slightly behind schedule, we decided to have an early start the next day, driving down to Gibraltar.

We had calculated; with a following wind, no breakdowns or major hold-up, we should hopefully reach Gibraltar by mid-afternoon.

The night was still and sultry, not a star to be seen in the inky-black skies. It felt as though a storm was slowly gathering, binding its time, waiting for the right moment to break.

At the first sign of rain, we folded up the table and chairs, slipped them under the van, then climbed into the van, which wasn't a moment too soon. The heavens opened, and in a matter of minutes the whole area around us resembled a lake.

A few young lads who were in a tent opposite us took advantage of it, lying flat on their backs, doing what looked like snow angels. In their case, water angels, while another one jumped up and down, water splashing around his exposed legs.

Chapter Fifteen

The following morning, we all woke up refreshed. It was the last leg of the trip before ending up, hopefully, in Morocco.

We didn't bother with breakfast as we were still full from last night's meal.

We set off as the very first glimmers of the rising sun were beginning to bleed through the lower edges of the darkness, as we pushed hard along the empty road, the head-lights flooding the way ahead.

Once we had passed Marbella, we came across the old village of San Roque that overlooked Gibraltar in the distance.

I had read a bit about this village. It was established around 1700. Unfortunately, according to historians, in 1649 a quarter of the Gibraltar population perished from an epidemic, resulting in a number of residents retreating to the area of San Roque, surviving the outbreak, and still today, they class themselves as the original 'Gibraltarians'.

We then passed through a number of small villages of Campamento, then the border town of La Linea.

Andrew warned me about the queues of traffic trying to cross into Gibraltar, he also mentioned to me that there was nowhere to park the van in Gibraltar, so we found a dedicated motorhome spot in Spain that overlooked the Rock for 12 Euros a night.

As a precaution, we took all of our money from the safe as we didn't want the van to be broken into, and more importantly, our passports as we would need them crossing into Gibraltar.

We also made sure our back-up money was safely tucked away at the back of the oven.

And yes, before you ask, we didn't forget to take the money out of the oven before using it.

Fifteen minutes later we passed through the border without a problem, before entering into Gibraltar as foot traffic, crossing the single runway at Gibraltar airport.

The asphalt was slicked to a black mirror by the recent heavy rains.

Ensuring there wasn't an airplane taking off or landing, as you can't be too sure these days, we safely entered the town, the impressive Rock towering above us.

Now get this, the first thing we saw was a red telephone box outside a Morrison's supermarket, and as we walked up Main Street, a single red bus drove by.

I also noticed to my alarm that diesel at Morrisons was £1.24 a litre. When we left the UK, it was close to £2 a litre.

Certain countries create impressions before you actually get there: sometimes those impressions are by looking at pictures, which only gives you a small glimpse of what to expect.

Gibraltar was a prime example of that.

It was incredible to realise that after such a mammoth journey we had only taken four days to get here.

So began our short time in Gibraltar, letting the place draw us in, to lead us down whichever alleys it desired, and lose ourselves in what I can only describe as a small part of Great Britain. During our time in Gibraltar, we came across a Tesco, Next and M&S. Both sides of Main Street were lined with bars and restaurants full of people sitting, eating, chatting away, all enjoying themselves. Half an hour from the border, though, I'd almost forgotten I was in another country, because everything looked as though we'd just passed through a portal into London back in the 70s. It was like being back in England.

We carried on up Main Street, soaking up the atmosphere, before we started seeing the typical English pubs and endless coffee shops.

There was The Horseshoe, and according to Andrew, it was known as The Donkey's Flip Flop.

The Horseshoe

(The Donkey's Flip Flop)

Then the Royal Calpe and further on The Trafalgar Bar. I was immediately struck at how litter free the area was, the roads bright and shimmering as if the rain had washed everything clean. A quick glance down one of the side streets showed me a glint of blue water, which must be the harbour.

We soon found ourselves discovering little pockets of the town away from the main roads; narrow alleyways leading to tiny courtyard gardens with colourful plants in terracotta pots.

To me, the whole place felt surreal, as though we were taking a leisurely stroll through a small fishing village in England.

We'd only walked a short distance when low and behold, we came across a Burger King, Pizza Express, and a McDonald's.

Andrew suggested we take a steady walk around the Rock, before relaxing in Catalan Bay, where we could sit and relax with a cold beer with the East side of the Rock, towering behind us. Which we did.

Andrew also mentioned to me about 'Biancas' restaurant in Ocean Village, where the manager—Debbie was a close friend of his.

I'd mentioned this to the others as we were making arrangements for the holiday, suggesting we call in for a drink.

With that in mind, Steve took the opportunity of getting in touch with a family friend of his that he'd known for years, who'd lived in Kilwinning in Scotland, and was now living in Gibraltar; David Wilson (no relation), informing him that we'll be calling into Gibraltar this week, hoping he was free to meet up. David said he would make doubly sure he was available.

After finishing our drink, taking in the scenery, Steve texted David, informing him that we were making our way to Biancas, which we found easily after a short walk, hoping Debbie was in the restaurant.

Steve had already sent David a couple of messages as we were making our way through Spain, updating him on our progress.

(Gibraltar is a British Overseas Territory located at the southern tip of the Iberian Peninsula and has an area of 2.6 sq. miles, so there was no way of us getting lost. It was home to over 32,000 people.

As you may now have guessed by this time, the landscape is dominated by the Rock of Gibraltar).

As we stepped inside the impressive restaurant, the room dappled in sunlight, I noticed a woman staring over me, standing behind the bar.

Her face lit up as she stepped out from behind the bar, walking towards me, saying, 'Andrew, what a surprise I . . . ." She stopped mid-sentence, suddenly realising I wasn't my brother.

I smiled at her, offering my hand out to the puzzled looking lady.

I said I was sorry to disappoint her; I was Andrew's good looking, older brother, which caused a few titters from the other four. Cheeky sods.

While enjoying her company, and may I add, eating an assortment of the restaurant's favourite Tapas, we mentioned to Debbie about our first holiday in 1969, and the reason for this one.

I'm not a fan of tapas, or as I call it, finger food, but it was delicious. We offered to pay but she wouldn't hear of it. She said it was her treat.

While we were all tucking into the food, chatting away, Steve kept glancing over towards the entrance, hoping to see David coming through the door.

He didn't have to wait too long, as he appeared moments later. Steve introduced him to us all; Geoff and myself had already met him and his wife last year when we visited Steve and Jean in Scotland.

David gave Debbie a hug and a kiss, as though they were long lost friends.

While David was chatting away to the others, Debbie enlightened me about Andrew's boozy nights, while working and living in Gibraltar.

I even sent over a text, telling Andrew that we had arrived at the bar, getting all the juicy gossip from Debbie.

I won't tell you what he sent back; children might be reading.

I also mentioned to Debbie, that Andrew had booked flights to Gibraltar, staying for three weeks during the school holidays, but I couldn't tell her when exactly.

Soon, it was time for us to leave, so we said our goodbyes to Debbie, before wandering around the narrow streets of Gibraltar.

After the coolness of the inside of the restaurant, the air outside felt like dragon's breath.

The sun had rose higher in the sky, bathing the buildings around us in a soft, shimmering light.

David suggested we call into Bruno's bar, which was only 30 metres from Biancas, so he could show us the stunning views from the bar.

He was correct, the views from the bar were amazing, the contrast with the heat and dazzling light of the outside struck me physically. Inside, it was cool, the thick walls keeping out the summer sun.

The water in the harbour looked crystal clear, fading to a deeper blue as it stretched away.

The dappling of sunlight and shadows highlighted the million pound plus yachts as they bobbed up and down on the clear blue water.

Sun-tanned, long-legged women were posing on the decks, taking selfies, flaunting their curves, wearing bikinis that resembled dental floss, leaving very little to the imagination, accentuating their hips and legs.

There was also a floating casino in the distance, which looked more like a cruise ship.

David said he would tag along with us to the border, going over old times when Steve managed the football team David played in, along with Steve's son Ritchie.

David pointed out to us that he'd developed both his friendship and footballing skills through Steve's help and guidance.

I could tell from the way he was expressing himself, that David had a great deal of time for Steve, adding that Steve and Jean were his most favourite people in the world.

From what I could gather from the conversation, David had a strong knowledge of a variety of sports from his time as a Royal Navy Physical Trainer, where he spent 24 years in physical education, before ending up in Gibraltar. He also had an amazing career in football, playing in Steve's young team, before becoming the national team manager for Gibraltar.

During his time as team manager, he led the squad against world champions Germany, Croatia, and his native Scotland at Hampden Park where Gibraltar scored their first ever competitive goal.

That said, after managing the national team for a short while, he took on the role as head coach for The Bruno's Magpies football team in Gibraltar.

As you can now well imagine, David is somewhat of a media celebrity on the TV, analysing and commentating games, his nickname being the Gary Neville/Jamie Carragher of Gibraltar.

He's also a well-known sports reporter.

Davie, as Steve called him a few times, was full of enthusiasm. *"I love the buzz of sports reporting and knowing that I can start an interview with deep interest in my subject, which excites me."*

Sorry I'm rambling on, but hey, come on. It's not every day you get to meet a celebrity in the flesh.

It was at that point, I asked him if he was available to take on the role of manager for the England team. I'm only joking. I didn't want to insult him.

The five of us could have listened to David for hours, but we had other plans, so as we got closer to the border, Geoff went online to check out the easiest route to get to Morocco, which read:

Algeciras is a port in the South of Spain.

It's not the most attractive city as it's a highly industrial place, so not somewhere you necessarily want to visit or hang around in.

That said, it is fairly easy to access and offers some of the quickest crossings to North Africa, which makes it a popular choice. Sailings from this part of Spain to Tangier Med only takes around 2 hours.

Since Morocco is out of the EU, travelling here is a little different. And when you board the ferry, you are handed a form to fill in.

This is for immigration purposes, where you may be asked further questions while you are on board, about why you are visiting Morocco, and where exactly you intend to visit.

While we were talking it over, David mentioned to us that the Spanish research firm (SECEGSA) had announced that the construction of the Morocco-Spain tunnel, which has been under consideration since 1979, will be able to proceed in 2030.

With a length of 42 km between terminal stations, including a 27.8 km underwater portion, this fixed line will connect the shores of both countries through the Strait of Gibraltar, which he said would attract more tourists to Gibraltar, and boost the economy, which by the looks of certain areas, needed it.

After a brief debate between the five of us, we decided not to go to Morocco, as it looked too much bother, so we bought a couple of postcards to remind us of our trip.

At least, with the tunnel being built, there's always the next time for us to finally visit Morocco.

With David's help, we did manage to go to Europa Point where we could see North Africa, which was as close as we were going to get to Morocco.

At that point, we finally reached the border, before saying our goodbyes to David, then heading back to the van.

Europa Point

Soon, Gibraltar was far behind us as we headed into open country with breath-taking views of blooming crimsons and purples, the sinking sun spanning a vast area from one end of the horizon to the other.

Now onto Lloret de Mar, which we'd worked out, would take us at least 14 hours non-stop.

After a small discussion we all agreed that we would chance it, hoping the roads wouldn't be as busy, and with only a couple of rest stops on the way, each of us taking it in turns with the driving.

At half past midnight, no light shone on the hillside save for the sliver of moon, and not a single electrical source for a dozen miles in any direction.

The next fourteen hours went like a flash, with no holdups, or diversions ...

Moments later, we were heading to what we all wanted to visit for a few days, reminiscing about Lloret de Mar . . .

Chapter Sixteen

It was a brilliant first morning at the campsite, in Lloret, knowing we would be hanging out together, having a laugh, relaxing, and having several drinks in the sun for a few days.

The campsite we had chosen when we were putting the holiday together was the Camping Lloret Blau, which was open all year round.

This particular campsite stood out above the rest, as it had over 200 pitches, with varying degrees of shade.

Most of the amenities were situated in the same general area, which was handy, which included a bar with a terrace overlooking an attractive outdoor swimming pool, bordered by a well-kept grassy sun terrace.

Within minutes, I'd done a reconnaissance wander around the camp site, noting where everything was located – especially the launderette, as I knew we would at some point need to wash and dry some of our clothes.

The toilet block, knowing being just the one in the van wasn't adequate, especially first thing in the mornings, and the on-site supermarket, which I found out later that it catered mostly for visiting tourists like ourselves. The shelves were lined with a large assortment of wine and beer, fresh fruit and vegetables, suntan lotion, which I didn't need. *I could probably sell some of mine to them if they ran short of it*, and beach toys and barbecue charcoal. In addition, there was a restaurant (with takeaway food), a well-stocked supermarket, as I'd already pointed out. WIFI, and a tourist information centre.

There was also a separate picnic area with benches close to the entrance to the site.

We'd arrived around 6 o'clock that morning.

Most of us took a nap while we could on the way, yet ensuring that at least one of us was awake, talking to the driver, making sure they didn't go to sleep at the wheel.

Once it's light, I find it difficult to sleep, so I left the others to catch up on their sleep.

The smell of bacon cooking drifted over the hedge bordering the van.

I casually walked towards it and peered through a small gap. In the pitch next door, there was a young couple making their breakfast.

It was a welcoming aroma to the site, which made my mouth water.

It was still early; yet it promised to be a hot June day.

I love watching towns wake up. Lloret wasn't any different.

There was a whole world out there, just waking up and I was a small part of it.

Sunrise in Lloret

Once I left the campsite I had the town to myself: it was just me and a few guys delivering crates of freshly-baked bread, and a couple of droning street-cleaning machines.

Then all at once things got frantic: the whole town suddenly came to life.

Row upon row of cafes and kiosks were opening, waiters setting out tables and chairs on the pavements.

Lloret was exactly as I remembered it.

The noise, the intoxicating aromas, the town coming alive.

As is often the way when you revisit somewhere you've been before, the allure maybe not the same and not as you remembered. In my case, it was the complete opposite. It was everything I remembered and more so.

One of the marvels when visiting other countries is the discovery that the world could be so full of variety, that there were so many different ways of doing essentially identical things, like eating relaxing and drinking.

(For those who aren't acquainted, Lloret de Mar, is a town on the Costa Brava in Spain's Catalonia region, is known for its Mediterranean beaches.

The medieval hilltop Castle of Sant Joan, to the east, offers views over the whole area, while the central Iglesia de Sant Roma church provides examples of both Catalan Gothic and modernist architecture.

On a cliff overlooking the sea, the Santa Clotilde Gardens were built in the style of the Italian Renaissance).

We had managed to find a decent pitch in the shade, under a line of trees, so that it wouldn't get too hot in the van and in the tent during the day.

By the time I'd returned to the van, the others were up and dressed in shorts and T-shirts, sitting around the table, eating freshly baked baguettes they'd bought at the supermarket, all of them on their phones, texting.

I'd already texted June as I was walking around the town, informing her I would call her sometime this evening.

I quickly joined them at the table, spreading a decent amount of jam on my Baguette, and drinking a large mug of freshly   ground   coffee,   Steve   had   made.

Chapter Seventeen

Once breakfast was over, we cleared away the dirty plates and knives, putting the jam in the fridge, before packing together a few items for the beach in one of the backpacks.

By mid-morning we were making our way to the beach.

As expected, the Santa Cristina Playa beach, which we had used on numerous occasions, was looking clean and well kept, along with the sparkling sand that was being washed away by crystal clear waters.

Just another day in paradise . . .

The view over the coast was magnificent, the stretch of deep blue sea beyond so vast and overwhelming that I felt as if I could walk into it from where I was stood. It was already shaping up to be a glorious day, the early sun a vibrant orange, its rays shifting the blue sea to a high-sparkle setting, along with a few wispy clouds drifting overhead. We knew that this particular beach had many areas of great interest for divers, especially the rocky headlands close by, which some of the lads visited last time.

In fact, if you are interested, there is a picture of Steve cliff diving from this particular headland, in the Morocco book.

The beach had a delightful promenade with scenic views of the Mediterranean, including several bars and restaurants.

The Mediterranean was a brilliant, sparkling blue, small waves whipped up by a gentle onshore breeze that brought a note of coolness to the merciless sunshine.

In the distance, there must have been at least a dozen surfers in the sea; shiny black figures with slashes of brilliant colours beneath them, heading into or out of the waves, some catching a large swell as it rolled in towards the shore, following it through and then falling, in a splash of foam, as the wave dispersed.

While the others relaxed on their towels, I spent ten minutes rubbing suntan lotion all over my legs, arms, and face.

If anyone had attempted to hug me, I would have probably shot up in the air like a rocket. I didn't have to ask one of them to rub some in on my back, as like me, they could remember the excoriating pain from the sunburn I was in the last time, and I had no intentions of repeating it. I also remembered to put some on the back of my legs so I wouldn't spend the rest of the holiday walking around like I needed to poo.

If anyone reading this had the discomfort of sunburn, you will know what I mean, which at all costs must be avoided.

Yet there was a time when we didn't have the awareness that sunburn was the slightest bit bad for us, let alone sometimes terminally grave for us.

Over the years, you would see young woman spreadeagled on the sands with sheets of tin foil underneath them, or under their chins, in the vain hope that it would intensify the sun's rays, making them brown more quickly. The other common method back in those days, which I'd heard about, was to rub yourself with cooking oil, so that you might fry like an egg, even in the privacy of your own back garden.

It's all changed now, with thousands of Tanning shops where for a few pounds a session, you can try and get brown by lying on a sun bed, which in my mind, was worse than using tin foil. These days, there have been so many alarming stories about the dangers of sunbeds that it is a wonder anyone still does it, although there's nothing new about the relationship between the British and that fiery orange mass of hydrogen and helium that increasingly we are not a hundred percent sure of whether to seek or avoid, which in fact was best summed up by the late Noel Coward in his most famous song, written in 1931.

Mad dogs and Englishmen go out in the midday sun.

The Japanese don't care to, the Chinese wouldn't dare to.

Hindus and Argentines sleep firmly from twelve to one,

But Englishmen detest a siesta,

In the Philippines there are lovely screens,

To protect them from the glare,

In the Malay states there are hats like plates,

Which the British won't wear,

At twelve noon the natives swoon, and

no further work is done,

But Mad Dogs and Englishmen go out in the midday sun.

***

I'm not what you could call a sun worshiper like the others, so after an hour, I decided to go for a walk down the beach, leaving the others to top up their tans, whispering to them not to lose sight of the backpack.

I walked towards the rocks, around the headland, passing toddlers tottering across the hot sand in disposable nappies sagging with sea water, girls with stomach piercings, glinting against tanned skin, lads in long trunks down to their shins, playing beach football, before encountering to my surprise, an isolated community of nudists who politely nodded hello.

What did surprise me, was the number of children romping naked in small pools by the rocks, which alarmingly, was growing crowds of puzzled looking people.

I could imagine the gullies being studded with small crabs and urchins that were almost never exposed.

It would be like having a glimpse of the seabed without having to put on a wetsuit.

A large wave broke, spraying the children with droplets of sea water, causing the naked children to scream with excitement, before running back to their parents.

I'm pretty certain I heard someone say in English, 'that's primitive', which was one of the kinder comments, while another voice said, 'they must be German'.

As we all know, the vast majority of adults in Germany have no qualms about undressing in public. Or in other words, exhibitionists – you choose.

Even the ones walking away from the scene were tut-tutting under their breath or shaking their heads in disgust.

Others just shot dirty looks at the parents.

Having said that, the German folk are what's now known as being a free spirit, which could hardly be said for the British.

When our two sons were growing up, we never thought twice about letting them go naked on a beach, if it was warm enough, so it was a shock to the system to realise that we were challenging some kind of unwritten protocol.

More shocking was still to think that people were sexualising our children, which by looking at the ones around me, were.

What though was weirder? Was very young children innocently playing naked on a beach, in the sun, or people being seriously affronted by the sight of small children innocently playing naked on the beach, especially with their parents, who thought it was the norm these days, and didn't care less, or even bat an eyelid.

Anyhow, that was my cue to head back, as I felt overdressed in a T-shirt and shorts.

I retraced my steps, this time walking up to my shins in the crystal blue waters.

At this point, I was beginning to tire.

By the time I'd reached the four of them, they said they'd had enough, wanting to find a bar, relax and have an ice-cold beer or two.

There was objection from me, and soon, we were heading towards the promenade.

We'd only walked a short distance when we came upon the Orient Express Café and Restaurant.

Luckily for us, there was two couples getting up from their table, which we casually sauntered over, hoping we didn't have to book a table, especially outside.

We didn't and before we knew it, there was waiter standing by the side of us, taking our order.

We all knew what we wanted to drink, so we ordered five pints of lager.

By mid-afternoon, after two pints of lager each, we made our way back to the van to freshen up for the night, and if anyone fancied a power nap.

I stayed in the luke-warm shower for a long time, and even though the water that was pattering against my tender skin of my face, arms, and chest it was soothing.

By the time we'd all showered, there was little time to sleep, so we sat and talked for an hour, once again reminiscing about old times, going over what we did in our teens, going to the Mecca in Bradford, and the holiday in Cornwall, reminding each other of several embarrassing occasions best forgotten . . .

Chapter Eighteen

It was late evening, the sky a rich blue high above, the setting sun lighting up the horizon like molten gold.

We couldn't wait any longer to get into the town and visit the only nightclub that was still in business after all these years – The Revolution!

As expected, the town came to life.

Brightly coloured lights criss-crossed the space above our heads, giving off a warm glow against the long shadows of approaching dusk.

Fire jugglers and street musicians were drawing in ice-cream-eating crowds, especially, wide-eyed children.

The air had a golden quality to it, the evening light soft, and honey warm as the sun sank towards the hills.

In the murmur of bars, all mixed with the pulse of the music, men were handing out flyers trying to entice people into their bars and night clubs.

We weren't interested because we knew where we were going for the night.

The outside of the Revolution hadn't changed in the slightest.

As we entered the club, I was suddenly transported back fifty-years. The atmosphere and the energy inside was electrifying, which felt the same, and as before we had to fight our way to the bar.

That was the reason we came here, reliving the past. Why not? There was one thing that I did notice that stood out; the sound of the music; it wasn't as deafening.

Then I remembered I hadn't put my hearing aids in.

I may have not been deafened by the volume, but I could certainly feel the vibrations through the souls of my shoes.

Oh! Didn't I mention that I'm partially deaf? I must be losing my memory as well.

I tend to wear them when I'm watching the TV, if not the volume would be turned up so loud, the people on the other side of the Mersey, in Liverpool would be able to hear what I was watching.

I didn't think of it at the time. If I'd had my hearing aids in, the noise would have been uncomfortable.

The other thing we noticed that had changed in Spain was the small amount of Bacardi they gave you in your drink.

Over the years the bar owners must have cottoned on and were now using optics instead of pouring spirits into glasses as though there was no tomorrow. The good thing though, a pint of beer/lager was around the €3 mark.

Having spoken to one of the bar staff at The Revolution, we were told to our delight that The Western Saloon, which we drank most nights in 1969, was now called The Gotham, and in the same building, with different owners.

We'd had enough after spending a couple of hours in Revolution, so made our way back to the van, deciding we would call into the Gotham tomorrow night for a change of scenery.

With more than 300 entertainment clubs, Lloret de Mar is a true paradise for party animals!

You could therefore say that Lloret de Mar is the ultimate nightlife capital of the Costa Brava, perhaps in Europe, where you can find a café, club or disco that is open 24/7! To say that you can have fun in Lloret de Mar by going out is an understatement! It's a holiday destination that never sleeps. There is something to do at every moment of the day.

We've been there, done it, and worn the T-shirt. All we wanted was a carefree holiday without going over the top.

We noticed over time, that nothing much had changed. Every restaurant was full, and the bars we passed were bursting at the seams.

As dusk approached, the streets and alleyways bubbled with life, the bars and restaurants filling up. Love-struck couples stuck together like glue. Families paraded together, from grandmothers in black shawls down to the smallest children.

As we entered the campsite, we spotted a video games room, which as you can imagine, we checked out.

We were also aware of the staff warning everybody as they entered the site that a storm was brewing and to make sure all tents were securely fixed, and belongings, such as table and chairs locked away, and any clothes hanging on washing lines.

As we entered the games room, we were amazed to see line after line of video machines, and can you believe it, there was an old-fashioned Pacman game and one that I could never get the hang of; Manic Miner.

While we were engrossed in the fun, we heard a squall of activity outside and all over the campsite. Rain was now rattling down, sounding like marbles landing on a tin roof.

Steve popped his head out to check what the fuss was all about. From where we were standing, he didn't look too happy, so we stopped what we were doing and went across to see what was happening outside. By this time the rain was blowing into the entrance of the games room.

The staff had been correct about a storm. The sky had darkened to almost black.

More rain poured down out of the sky in thick, steady drops. Water sheeted from the gutters from the other buildings, flowing in rivers over the ground.

In the distance, we could hear caravan awnings being winched in, windows slammed shut, parents shouting for their children to get inside this minute, while other people hurried about around their tents and caravans, hastily gathering their towels and clothes from washing lines, and families herding their young children into their tents, caravans, and vans.

Because the ground was dry, the pitter, patter of rain on the hard earth sounded almost like metallic.

Each raindrop sparked up a plume of dust so fine it looked like steam was rising from the ground.

Then in the distance, a low rumble of thunder began rolling towards the camp site.

The start of a decent storm was brewing.

Steve looked over at us all, asking us if we'd checked the guy ropes on the tent before coming out?

I hadn't. I thought the others had.

Forgetting about being soaked to the skin, the five of dashed towards the motorhome and the tent, hoping it hadn't been blown away, the rain cutting sidelong into our faces.

With every clap of thunder, we physically jumped, and at every lightning strike, we winced.

When we reached our spot, we found the tent being pulled off the ground by the strong wind, and to our horror, there was a young boy hanging onto one of the guy ropes, trying to stop the tent from flying away.

The funny thing was, he was laughing his head off at the top of his voice.

We all dashed over, to help the boy, while at the same time his father appeared from his caravan, giving us a helping hand.

Then it happened.

A big gust of wind suddenly sprung up, causing the guy ropes to slowly come away from the ground, resulting in the young boy being lifted off his feet.

I quickly let go of the rope I was holding, reached up and grabbed hold of the boy around his waist.

With the aid of Geoff, we managed to safely pull him back down to earth.

God knows what would have happened to the boy if I hadn't grabbed hold of him. Doesn't bear thinking about.

Can you believe it, the boy was still giggling away to himself?

Along with the rest of them, I was struggling to keep the tent from flying off into the distance. I was clinging onto the guy rope for dear life.

By this time, the tent looked like an oversized kite in the sky.

After fighting against the strong wind for a short while, we somehow managed to get the tent back on the ground, before we swiftly folded it up as best, we could, knowing that the sleeping bags inside would make it difficult to keep it flat.

Due to the tent being soaking wet and knowing there wasn't sufficient room in the van to store it, and more importantly, leaving wet patches on the carpet, we decided to erect the tent.

It took us ten minutes of struggling, trying like mad to get the pegs into the muddy ground. Satisfied that the tent pegs were firmly fixed in the ground, and because it was my son's tent, it was only right that I slept in it that night, preventing it from blowing away, rather than in the warmth of the van, which I didn't mind, plus it would give the others more room.

Meanwhile the boy's father was giving him a telling off.

After we realised what had happened, we all burst out laughing, including the father.

Especially after someone in the crowd called out asking if anyone had caught the bizarre incident on their mobile phone.

Can you believe it, no one did, as they were more worried about the boy?

By this time, what little hair we had looked like rat's tails. We couldn't have been any wetter.

After thanking the boy for his bravery, he along with his father went inside their caravan away from the continuous rain, while we went inside the van to dry ourselves, and to change out of our wet clothes.

I was chilled to the bone and dripping wet.

It was while we were drying ourselves, I mentioned about the time in France when we were parked up in a tiny village, in a storm, where a tree close by was struck by lightning.

After thinking about it for a few seconds, the image suddenly came back to them.

Once dry, we made ourselves a cup of coffee, relishing the comforting warmth of the mug in my hands.

After finishing the mug of coffee, placing it in the sink with the others, I left the van, wishing them all a goodnight, before crawling on my hands and knees into the tent. I also took a pair of wellington boots into the tent just in case I needed to go to the toilet through the night.

The only saving grace, was that the inside of the tent was bone dry due to the sewn-in ground sheet.

You know what, there is an incredible snug, peaceful feeling to falling asleep to the sound of rain pattering off canvas just inches from you face.

Three hours later, the weather still raged, as I watched the flashes of lightening through the canvas of the tent.

Years ago, when on a family holiday in southern France, we got caught up in storm to end all storms.

And to make sure, if for some reason the tent flew off, we packed all of our clothes in our suitcases, so if we did wake up in the morning, in the open air, we would only have to look for our suitcases, instead of searching the camp site for our clothes.

Chapter Nineteen

The storm picked up a pace around midnight. The thunder was becoming louder, circling the area, before doing its worse.

All night the wind still raged.

The wind was ferocious, so much so, the tent frame was complaining with the strain. It was billowing so much, to the point where the poles were almost bending in half.

I just laid there on my back with my feet firmly pressed against the sides of the tent, with my arms spread as wide as possible, using my weight, doing anything in my power to stop the tent from blowing away again.

The sides rattled, no longer a flap, just a terrible racket as if someone was shaking stones in a tin can. I was now becoming worried that the guy ropes may loosen, causing the pegs to come out of the ground.

There was only one thing for it.

Go outside and check.

I slipped on the boots, before unzipping the tent door, the storm hitting me straight in the face.

The wind was so strong that it was almost impossible to walk.

Trying my best, I worked my way round the outside, checking the pole footings, then re-fixing the guy ropes, burying the pegs further into the ground, the boots squelching in the mud. Now open to the elements, I was wishing I'd stayed inside the tent. Just then, Steve opened one of the windows of the motorhome, asking if I was, okay?

I said I was fine, thanks.

I was just fixing the pegs, because some of them had worked loose, hoping the storm would soon pass.

The tent was now being thumped from all angles, and visibly straining from the assault.

The poles, creaking and whining, began to slowly vibrate as if trying to shake themselves loose from the canvas.

I gasped as the tent swayed violently to the left, then right, putting up one last fight before I finally managed to get the pegs firmly in place. I left the muddy boots outside, then crawled on my hands and knees back into the tent.

The storm got louder and louder through the course of the night.

What's that old saying – The rain in Spain, falls mainly on the plain? Well, in this case, it was raining stair rods on a camp site in the middle of Spain.

As the next day dawned, I awoke with a start.

Abruptly, as often happens when something extraordinary had happened the night before. Then it all came rushing back to me.

There had been no let-up in the storm, until around 5 o'clock, when I heard the chirping of the birds, as I emerged from the tent.

Wiping the sleep from my eyes, I took in the scene around me. Thankfully, the tent had not disappeared, along with me inside it, but it looked the worse for wear.

In the cold light of day, it looked as though a tornado had hit the campsite, not a storm

Inquisitive heads poked out of their caravans and tents, surveying the damage: chairs and tables tipped over, branches down.

I even spotted what was left of a tent stuck up in tree, flapping away in the breeze. Some poor sod will have to climb up to get it down.

The place looked a poorly site. It reminded me of a shanty town in a cowboy film.

It was if the wind had assumed a monstrous form, striding into the campsite, trying to tear as many tents as possible.

The storm had passed, the rain proving to be lingering, which meant that there would be no chance of getting anything dry.

It was still raining, but not as bad as last night.

The weather was in no mood for shifting; a dense, low sky smothered the horizon, dull monotone clouds for as far as the eye could see.

I had thought about taking a stroll towards the supermarket. I got no more than a hundred yards before I turned back by the downpour, waiting for the damn thing to stop.

An hour later the rain, thank goodness, had finally stopped, so I headed down to the camp shop to fetch us all croissants.

Minutes later, the sun revealed a world that remembered nothing of the night before, save for a few puddles and damp pavements.

I sucked in a deep breath of cool fresh air and held it in my lungs, looking around me, watching the other campers making their way to the beach, all laden with towels, ice boxes and bags stuffed full of sun lotions.

The high, bright sun added an extra layer of charm to the campsite.

Before calling into the supermarket, I called into the toilets to spend a penny and wash my hands and face.

Looking in the mirror, I noticed that I had bags under my eyes and no matter how much cold water I splashed on my face I still thought I looked bleary. What did I expect after having no sleep for nearly twelve hours? By the time I'd finished, the sun had popped up surprisingly, as things do when you wait for it long enough to forget what you were waiting for in the first place.

Chapter Twenty

Following on from our late breakfast we ventured to the site's supermarket to buy a few bottles of water along with a couple of day-old English newspapers, before continuing towards the beach.

An hour later we were sitting on the beach in the sunshine, the wind in my hair, the crystal clear Med in front of us. The scents of saltwater and fish floated in the air, the wind caressing every bit of my exposed, sun-warmed skin.

We all remarked that the road to the beach was the quietest we'd ever seen it. No sign of any Brits, no booming club music and no quad bikes zooming up and down the promenade.

I just stood and gazed at the water, soaking up my surroundings.

An inflatable yellow speedboat was cutting through the waves, and what looked like a fishing boat further towards the horizon, nothing more than a pale smudge amongst the glittering blue water.

Before we tried out the beaches, we re-acquainted ourselves with the restrictions I'd printed off the internet :-

Men walking around with their shirts off or women wearing only bikinis or swimwear, could be fined €300. At all Spanish beach showers, it is illegal to wash with soap and shampoo and you can be fined up to €750 if caught doing so.

Camping on the beach is also against the law and could result in the same fee having to be paid. After a successful pilot scheme last year, the Spanish government is expanding a no-smoking policy across popular beaches in Spain.

If you are found smoking at a smoke-less beach, you will be fined €30. Cigarette smoke and 'butts' can be a real menace for non-smokers and children building sandcastles.

*The beach is also considered a public place, and as nice as it is to drink beer in the sun, **it is not allowed**, unless you go to a beach bar and consume the drink at one of the tables there.*

That said, people do it and get away with it, yet being a party of 16, you will attract attention!

Let's be honest, the beaches in Spain are nothing like the ones in the UK, when the sun makes an unexpected appearance after being on holiday for a week sheltering from the rain in the amusement arcades.

What you see on the beach on a warm summer's day in the UK is the extraordinary variety of unfolding activities; the game of Frisbee, cricket, football, paddle-tennis, catch, children burying their dads up to their necks in the sand, dads making sand racing cars and rowing boats, hoping to keep the young ones entertained for hours.

Oh, and not forgetting families trying to make the biggest sandcastle.

Fully dressed old men and women paddling in the sea, the woman screaming when they spotted something undesirable floating towards them.

Trying to erect a windbreaker on windy days, which was most days.

Let's not forget, walking back to the car because you had forgotten little Jimmy's bucket and spade, also dashing to the loo.

Not to mention the number of people wriggling into their swimsuits under a towel that was only just large enough to cover their private parts.

Yep, relaxing in Spain was what the doctor ordered.

What clouds there were, soon cleared the horizon in seconds, drenching the waves blood-red, and over to our right was the Castell d'en Plaja.

The five of us had been keeping ourselves to ourselves quietly reading and listening to music on our i-phones for an hour when suddenly a group of yobs old enough to buy alcohol legally in England began playing football in front of us in a bid to impress a group of girls sunbathing over to our right.

I thought it was too good to be true when the lads started playing football. I had spoken too soon.

Steve then pointed out to us, that was us fifty years ago.

We all agreed. The thing that was worse; was when I looked around us. I could see that we were the odd ones out.

That's when Nigel piped up saying it was because of our age, and good looking.

Both, we all called out, resulting in us all rolling about on the sand, laughing.

Within minutes the beach was crowded, splayed with tanned and the beautiful, the topless and the should-be topless, laid out on carefully arranged deck chairs, along with lines of impaled lopsided parasols in the sand you had to pay an arm and a leg to sit underneath.

I was the whitest person in sight, apart from my legs.

Then the inevitable happened. The young guys started to get more rowdy, pestering the young girls, who just wanted to be left alone.

From where I was sitting, I could see that the lads had been hiding cans of beer under their beach towels.

Not a good sign.

I could tell that things were going to turn ugly.

A hot climate, fuelled with cheap booze, and pretty girls in bikinis wasn't the right combination.

I have to say, the girls took it in their stride, basically telling them to bugger off, and to leave them alone, also adding that their boyfriends were meeting them in an hour.

That last piece of important information suddenly resulted in the drunken lads to make a hasty retreat.

We knew that this time of the year they would be a large amount of 'younger' people.

That didn't put us off as we were young once. Thank goodness for that, as I don't think either of us was prepared to let the young lads intimidate the girls, even though they could probably kick the shit out of us.

The lads I mean, not the girls, or maybe they could, you never know.

We just wanted a peaceful holiday, relaxing in the sun.

I have to admit, in our teens we had done silly things, but not harassing the opposite sex.

Once we were satisfied that there wouldn't be any more trouble, we started to relax a little.

As I reflected back in the old days, camping, as we knew it then had changed over the years, with the rapidly growing middle-class interest in camping has also given rise to the phenomenon of 'glamping', a contraction of 'glamorous camping', by which you sleep in a canvas structure.

To me this seems contrary to the whole spirit of camping, slumming it.

There's nothing like putting up a tent in the dark, struggling with the guy ropes, swearing at the tent pegs as you try to get them in the rock hard ground, an essential and possibly even rewarding part of the experience.

As I found to my cost last night.

For my money, if camping doesn't involve at least a little bit of hardship, it's not proper camping.

Having said all that, I was now changing my tune, because living in the motorhome was a sheer delight, even though I was sleeping in the tent most nights.

I can now understand that one of the greatest thrills of having a motorhome or a camper van is the freedom to make snap decisions about where you would be waking up in the morning. Constantly shifting the shape of your adventure, day after day, week after week, month after month . . .

The only routine I have at the moment, is deciding what time to get up in the morning, and what to do that day.

Another reason holidaying in a motorhome or a camper van, rather than of a tent, is that you don't have be careful where you pitch your tent, because in 1969 we pitched one of the tents on an ants nest. We wondered at the time why the pitch was empty.

Or if the site was full, you would end up setting up camp in the next field in a bad spot. Then waking up in the morning with your tent and legs being sucked under a combined harvester.

Plus, the sorrow of finding out that giant hornets love nothing more than the smell of your mosquito repellent.

I was also glad we weren't flying, especially after the delays and queues at Manchester airport during the early part of summer.

Hundreds of travellers described the situation as a "shambles" and "appalling" with some forced to queue for up to six hours. I heard that some travellers have faced long queues for check-in and security since the middle of March with some missing their flights.

Various factors had been blamed for the delays, which has also affected Heathrow and Stansted airports, including staff shortages and a spike in demand for travel. I read that families were sleeping on airport floors only to find that their flights had been cancelled. Conditions were described as 'like a zoo' at one terminal, while some passengers who did manage to fly were told that their luggage had been sent elsewhere.

That would have been a total disaster for us five old gits.

And owing to the delays and cancellations at most UK airports, I would assume more people will now use the ferry, knowing there would be less delays, which we found to our relief at Dover.

After watching the testosterone fuelled lads antics for the last hour, it became apparent that they weren't going anytime soon, so we decided to wander into the town for a drink in one of the bars.

Fifteen minutes later we were drinking beer outside one of the many sports bars.

A local team were playing in a charity match, but please don't ask me who their opponents were. The local team supporters were out in force, filling the bar to the rafters, standing on chairs outside to get a better view of the TV.

Surprise, surprise, we stayed until around 11 o'clock that night, drinking, and eating home-made Pizzas, with garlic bread, which were delicious, and by the end of the night, watching the supporters celebrating after their win.

Chapter Twenty-One

By the time we'd returned to the campsite, the heat inside the tent was unbearable: it was like being in a pressure cooker, the hot, dead air stifling.

The sun was flickering like a flame above the horizon, the stars and moon already so bright that we could clearly see our way back to the van.

I decided to take a walk around the campsite, slowly drinking a bottle of beer I'd taken from the fridge, listening to the nocturnal chorus all around, the incessant chirp and buzzes of insects, plus a lonely cry of some night bird (the feathery kind).

Dim lights shone here and there in the tents, campervans, and fancy motorhomes, along with the sound of someone softly strumming a guitar in the distance, plus the constant hum of insects.

Looking up at the stars, I could see just a small part of the expanse of the universe. It felt so peaceful and tranquil.

Further on, I came to the swimming pool, the still water, shining silvery under the moonlight.

I moved closer to where the trees grew closer, the air cooler.

I stood there for a few minutes, recalling the good times, back in 1969.

Even though I say so myself, I have a good memory.

I can even remember one of my early childhood memories when I was three years old, living in Chesterfield, sitting cross-legged on the floor, in front of our black and white television the size of a tumbler drier on a screen the size of a dinner plate, watching the coronation of Queen Elizabeth II.

We were the only ones on a row of cottages that had a television, and I bet you can imagine, the number of neighbours, all wanting to sit and watch the ceremony, live.

But for the life of me, there are moments when I can't remember what I did last week. I'm also forgetful. I've lost count the number of times I have left the kitchen light on. That's old age for you.

The following day, we met up with a group of young guys from London in the campsite bar. They said they were travelling around Europe on a gap year in a large van that they had converted into a motorhome, which was full of musical instruments.

As we were chatting away, they invited us over to their van to listen to them play music that evening, which we said was a good idea.

We didn't move from the camp site that day, as we'd had enough of the beach, so we did our own thing, until it was time for tea, which was beans on toast for a change.

Nigel and Mike played a couple of games of chess, which Nigel had brought. Steve cleaned out the van.

Geoff and I did offer to help, but he said there was no need, thanks. So, Geoff read a magazine about football.

After updating the log, I relaxed on one of the chairs, reading the new Scott Mariani thriller on my Kindle.

Two hours later, we made our way over to the London guy's converted van, taking a long with us a couple of bottles of whisky, glasses, and a pack of beers which I'd bought at the supermarket that afternoon.

As I sat down, I noticed a few stickers on the side of their van, which brought back a few memories.

Some were unreadable, but the ones I could see must have been years old, such as – NO NUKES; STRAWBERRY FIELDS FOREVER; ALL I WANT IS TO LIVE IN A VAN AND SMOKE WEED. But the best one, was – PICKS UP FIVE TIMES MORE WOMEN THAT A LAMBORGHINI.

As we were chilling out outside their van, we heard a woman shouting in the distance. High and terrified . . .

Chapter Twenty-Two

We all stood, looking for the source of the screams before we all acted. We ran towards where the screams were coming from, nearly colliding with a young woman, her dirty face, streaked with tears.

She stopped screaming to catch her breath, as she tried to tell us that their tent had caught fire from a hot coal from their barbecue, quickly adding that her friend had dashed over to the reception, to make them aware of the fire.

The first thing I did was to ask her if she was hurt.

She shook her head, before grabbing me by the hand, dragging me towards where there was smoke coming from the other side of a caravan, the others close on my heels.

Others were running past us.

Someone was hollering for people to get buckets of water and form a line.

It was a curtain of flames, as we reached her tent. It was like a living thing. The smoke was thick, the fire spreading, the red-hot flames quickly licking from branch to branch on the trees and bushes behind the tent.

From the size of the fire, it must have been a four-man tent, as it took up a large size of the pitch.

The heat was immense, the smoke starting to clog the back of my throat. In the dull light everything gleamed garish, shadows playing across the ground, like a peculiar living tattoo.

Flames were also visible in the woods, creeping from one tree to the next, flaring and dancing in the muggy late evening.

The air above warped and billowed out of shape like streamers from the heat.

From somewhere over towards the main road, came the wailing two-tone siren of a fire engine.

It was then, when her friend appeared, her hands up to her mouth, shaking her head in despair.

Meanwhile, the fire danced on, smoke darkening against the dark blue sky.

The wind suddenly shifted, causing clouds of smoke to float towards us, burning our throats, blinking back tears.

My head began to pound from breathing in the smoke.

Someone was running back and forth from their caravan with a pot full of water, hoping to dowse out the raging fire, which was futile, as the fire was now well and truly out of control.

We all stared at the fire for a moment, mesmerised by the flames.

It could only have been five minutes, maybe less, before the fire engine pulled up by the side of what was left of the tent.

The firemen, in their dark blue protective suits and their bright yellow helmets, played their hoses over the remains of the tent, damping down the smouldering plastic and trees, along with lines of bushes that had been ablaze only minutes ago.

The fire was out now, along with the trees and the tent.

The surrounding area was thoroughly soaked to prevent any lingering sparks from restarting the flames.

A couple of firemen tramped through the woods behind the burnt trees, checking their work, making certain the seat of the fire was well and truly extinguished.

Nigel handed out bottles of water he'd brought back from the motorhome, the water sluicing the smoke from our throats, while the fire brigade went about their work.

One of the girls doubled over, bracing her hands on her thighs, and vomited onto the wet grass. Once she had stopped, Nigel handed her a bottle of water, which she took a swig from, spat it out, getting rid of the aftertaste, swilling her mouth out, before finishing the water. After thanking Nigel, she blew her nose a couple of times.

Once the firemen were happy that the fire was truly out, they rewound the hose, before ensuring both girls were uninjured, then jumped back in their vehicle then made their way back to the station.

I asked both girls if there was anything important in the tent, such as their passports, money, etc.

Staring at the black remains of their tent, they didn't at first seem to have heard me. Then the other girl showed me a small see-through zip-lock bag, with their passports and money inside.

She told me once the tent caught fire, she dashed into the tent, putting her own safety at risk to retrieve their personal belongings.

A brave, and stupid girl, but I kept that thought to myself.

Then they both burst into tears again, harsh caws escaping them.

People react differently towards an horrific accident. All I could do was to leave them to get it out of their system. After wiping away the tears, the one who shouted the alarm, told us that she watched in horror her friend disappear in the tent, into a rolling grey cloud of smoke.

Stammering, she said she kept shouting for her friend to get out, her eyes wide from the shock of what had just happened.

The two of them were beside themselves with grief, and frightened, their faces a mask of confusion, uncertainty, and fear.

I could see tears of grief in both of the girl's eyes, so I offered my tent for the rest of our holiday, along with my sleeping bag.

Steve chipped in offering his sleeping bag, as we had a spare blanket stored in the motorhome.

They thanked us, but after a short discussion between themselves they refused, saying it would be best if they headed back home.

At least there was one saving grace. The car was parked in the main car park.

Then there was long conversation with the girls and the staff of the campsite.

I could only hear snippets of the conversation, but what I did catch was that the staff said not to worry about the damage to the trees, informing them that they would take care of getting rid of what remains there was of their tent.

From where I was standing, it seemed to satisfy the girls.

Once the girls nerves had calmed down, they again thanked us for our generosity, before making their way to the car, and home.

We walked with them, making sure they were certain about going home.

By this time, they were insistent, saying that the holiday had been ruined, adding that they had little choice.

After waving them off, we headed off back to the van, as we'd had enough excitement to last us a week.

The air was thick with humidity, the clouds to our west casting the land into deep shadow.

Crickets filled the air with their soft burr as we meandered through the trees and caravans.

I knew it would take me ages to get to sleep, going over what could have happened if the girl had become trapped in the burning tent. Doesn't bear thinking about.

Relatively speaking, putting it in its correct context, "IF" is a big word.

Slouching outside the van, the smell of smoke coming off our hair and clothes, I thought I would lighten the mood.

I'd brought a book with me – Mangled English by Gervase Phinn, which I'd bough in a charity shop years ago.

I told them to sit back, relax and pin back their ears.

Which they did; glasses to their lips, sipping whisky from a bottle I couldn't even attempt reading the name of it.

I started off by reading a few unusual book titles such as:-

Handbook for the Limbless

Fishing for Boys

The Big Problems of Small Organs

A French Letter Writing Guide

And the funniest one as far as I was concerned was:-

Cataract Extraction Through the Back Passage

I then went on with some malapropisms:-

He's a wolf in cheap clothing

She's fluid in French you know

It serves ornamental food

The front tyre had flatulence

Then I finished off with a few Spoonerisms:-

If you're dirty, go and shake a tower

It's a lack of pies

The car had a bat flattery

Now this is the pun fart . . .

I could see at that point they were getting bored, but it was just a bit of fun.

Anyhow, Mike and Nigel went for a wander around the campsite, and to my surprise, Geoff settled down to finish reading one of my books; *9/11: Blank Canvas*. Steve was relaxing on a chair, trying a level 3 Sudoku.

By the expression on his face; finding it difficult, while I updated the holiday logbook.

After fifteen minutes, Steve gave it up as a bad job, putting the book and pencil away in his backpack, before rifling for his headphones, then fumbling with the metal end into the tiny hole in his mobile phone.

It took him two tries to secure the little white buds in his ears. Then all I heard was a tinny sound coming from his ears . .
.

Chapter Twenty-Three

The following morning, I woke up in the tent feeling like I was being roasted alive.

It was when we were setting the table for breakfast, we found a pack of beers lying on the ground outside the van with a big Thank You and a smiley face, drawn on top with a black felt-tip-pen.

We all presumed it was from the two girls.

Over the last few days, we'd noticed that Geoff was struggling when walking for a certain length of time, so we strongly suggested that when we went out today, we would take the wheelchair.

Especially after we'd decided to take a leisurely stroll along the coastal path the night before.

Geoff said he wasn't feeling up to it, but he said we should go, and he'd stay at the van so he could take it easy and read his book.

Mike then suggested that we took a boat ride for a change of scenery, which we all thought was a great idea.

Even Geoff said he was up for it.

Minutes later, we were heading for the port.

By the time we reached it, all of the fancy cabin cruisers and pontoon boats were all out at sea, which left us with a couple of inflatable ones.

We picked the one with a man who reminded us of Captain Haddock from the Tintin cartoons. Full, black beard, captains hat perched on his head, and a pipe hanging from the side of his mouth.

The boat was moored up by the side of a wooden ramp, that wasn't as sturdy as it might have been.

At least we'd soon get our sea legs.

The structure wobbled beneath our feet as we made our way to what I can only describe as an oversized dinghy. In fact, that's what it was.

There was room for at least twelve.

I leapt in, landing unsteadily, grabbing hold of the wooden seat to keep myself from falling completely.

As soon as the five of us had made ourselves as comfortable as possible on the wooden benches, the captain pulled out a metal box in the stern of the boat that was tucked under a slated seat next to the outboard motor. The captain, as we now referred him as, who smelled of seaweed, tipped the contents out on the bottom of the boat, before handing out lifejackets to us all, which smelled of fish.

Being only the five of us, it gave us a bit more room to move about on the wooden benches, and I couldn't see any more people wanting to get onboard. That said, the people walking past were taking a wide berth. I wondered why? I soon found out to our peril …

At that point, I should have known it wasn't going to be plain sailing.

The only other time I'd been on a boat of this size was when a few of us spent a holiday in Cornwall.

If I remember correctly, that didn't turn out as it should have done.

I wouldn't call myself a landlubber, but from where I was sitting, the sea looked a little choppy a few yards from the harbour walls.

I hadn't realised; I was squeezing the side of the seat with both hands with such force that my knuckles were turning white, and my palms were stinging from the pressure of my grip.

Peering over the side of the boat, tiny waves pushed it to and fro, making a soft whispering sound, just audible when the gulls decided to stop squawking for a moment.

With an unpleasant sneeze that could have been heard all over Lloret, the captain wiped his nose on the end of his sleeve before sitting down to cradle the tiller.

Needless to say, we didn't get off the boat.

In fact, we daredn't.

Before we knew it, the captain was casting off.

The conditions for what we hoped was a short boat ride seemed perfect – blue skies, calm waters – as we pulled away from the pontoon there was no reason to believe that everything was about to go drastically wrong.

We soon passed through the harbour walls, staring up, looking at the people dotted along its length, fishing rods and crab lines in their hands, plastic buckets by their feet.

Some of them even gave us enthusiastic waves in our direction.

There were others, mostly men, unshaven, squatting on the steps, some smoking, others drinking from tin cups.

I watched a young boy waving a fishing net in the direction of the harbour wall while his mother held onto him, not letting him get too close to the edge, while the dad helped a little girl pick up pebbles, putting them in her pink, castle-shaped plastic bucket, and a fisherman unloading crates from his boat a little way along the wall.

Before we knew it, we were in open sea, with a few sailboats darting back and forth and, in the far distance, a large tanker bound for who knows where, along with a number of fishing boats heading back to the port.

A few speedboats skimmed across the surface of the water while quieter, bobbing dinghies floated in the sea, and kite surfers trying to reach for the skies . . .

All about us dozens of seagulls hung in the unseen breeze, hoping we'll throw scraps of food for them.

For the next ten minutes or so, all was going steady, then behind us came a sudden bang. Startled, the five of us turned as one to see to our horror a thin plume of black smoke wafting up from the outboard motor, before the boat came to a bobbing halt. The motor then coughed and spluttered, then died.

From the resigned expression on the captains face, I suspected that this wasn't the first time the motor had given up the ghost.

After having pulled a small toolbox out from underneath the bench he was sitting on, he rummaged his thick, dirty fingers through a mess of what sounded like nuts and bolts, before pulling out a large screwdriver, which he was now using to undo the top of the motor unit.

While he was checking the motor, one of us, I'm not sure who it was, asked he could fix it. We didn't get a reply, just a grunt.

Chapter Twenty-Four

Meanwhile, we were slowly drifting on a strong current that was dragging the boat towards a flotilla of dinghies from the local sailing school, all trying to grasp the basics of seamanship.

Distracted by our predicament, we had failed to notice that we were now floating in the busy paths of the learner sailors.

All of a sudden there was a massive shunt, causing us to grab hold of our seats to steady ourselves, resulting in Geoff and Mike ungainly falling off their seats.

We had been rammed from the side by a young man, wearing thick glasses who, despite his teacher yelling at him, had completely failed to understand the difference between port and starboard.

So, instead of steering away, had run his boat into us.

Just at that moment, the captain yelled out at the top of his voice, for us to bail out, then grabbing the oars that were laid flat on the floor, before frantically attempting to row us back into the port before the boat sank.

The collision must have deflated the boat.

All we could find was a long pole with a brass hook on the end.

We didn't hesitate, plus the fact that we didn't have much choice in the matter.

The dinghy was sinking, fast.

So, we improvised by using our hands to bail out the water.

In the meantime, the captain was desperately trying to row the boat towards land, at the same time shouting for us to bail out quicker, which was easier said than done under the circumstances.

It was then when we resigned ourselves to the fact that at some point soon, we were all going to end up in the water.

Luckily for us, the lifejackets looked in a damn sight better condition than the engine.

Meanwhile, the five of us were bailing out like demons. We could see that we had so much to physically do, to get us safely back to dry land.

Water was now up to our thighs, due to us having to crouch down on our hands and knees to bail out the water, in our cold, cupped hands.

Our bodies, swayed from side to side, trying to keep our balance.

Besides the boat beginning to groan and tilt at an awkward angle, it was also deflating at a rate of knots. Pun not intended.

I could see the captain sweating with the effort, as he kept looking over his shoulder to see how far we had to go.

It was only a matter of yards.

At that moment, the boat was sinking lower with each stroke.

The pontoon was almost in reaching distance.

So, with one heaving pull of the oars, the captain ordered us to abandon ship, or in our case, abandon dinghy.

His voice was rising now in pitch. The five of us all reacted the same, hanging on for dear life to the side of the boat as long as humanly possible, before slipping over the side into the cold water.

I just hoped and prayed that there was no jellyfish in this part of the Mediterranean.

As we approached the harbour walls, I was able to look up at the fishermen who by this time had gathered to watch us as we swam our way back to dry land, all of them shouting encouragement. Even the little boy and girl were urging us on.

The battle was getting the better of me. That said, I had a morbid fear of water at the best of times. I was slowly floundering, while the other four swam with ease towards the pontoon.

I was treading water, at the same time trying to swim against the outgoing tide, because I wasn't sure if the lifejacket would keep me afloat by the time, I'd reached land.

In the meantime, the pontoon was full of eager helpers, all reaching out with their hands, trying to pull the six of us out of the water.

Minutes later, we all flaked out, trying to catch our breath, feeling exhausted.

We then turned back to the where the boat had been, only to see the sea water licking over the top of the boat, before sucking the whole thing down, to the murky depths.

There was only one thing to say to the captain; We'd like our money back please.

All things considered; he did ask us if we were okay. But it wasn't easy to sound calm and collected when your teeth were chattering away, and you couldn't stop shivering.

In spite of everything, we were all safe. We handed over the lifejackets to an embarrassed captain, then made our way to the nearest public toilets to ring out our wet clothes.

Wearing our damp clothes we made our way back to the camp site, for a well-earned drink, which we rightly deserved.

I recently read an article, saying that heavy drinkers were 'healthier and happier in later years'. I can't vouch for all of us about being healthier, but I can definitely say we were a damn sight happier.

We'd had enough excitement for one day, thank you, so after freshening ourselves up, changing into clothes that reflected what we were going to do, we sauntered into town for a slap-up meal, stopping at several watering holes on the way.

The Iglesia de Roma

For now, though, the evening sun continued to beat down with an intense heat, relentless Mediterranean heat that had slowly started to bake my skin as soon as I stepped in the sun.

The Iglesia de Roma church rose into the night sky, forming one side of the square while the little trio of boulangerie, boucherie and charcuterie were shuttered and dark on the other side.

The restaurant we had chosen was bright and busy. It had been recommended by the owner of the camp site, adding that the locals used it, but not to worry, saying jokingly, you won't be ushered into a private dining room complete with a washing machine and tumble dryer.

As it happened, we were directed to one of a dozen wooden tables arranged on the pavement. It was almost eight o'clock. The air was still warm, thick with the smells of ribeye steaks, rich sauces, Paella, combined with the distinctive bouquet of red wine.

Candles and glasses and half-empty bottles of beer soon lined our table, coupled with the distinctive musty smell of those revolting cigarettes the French smoke.

This was our first decent meal since we set off from the UK.

Ice-cold lagers arrived and the light-hearted banter continued during the course of the meal.

I also found that the Spanish were more easy-going than the citizens from other parts of Europe, more so the French, especially the ones in the north.

The Spanish tended to move and talk more slowly and generally calmer.

As expected, the meal was exceptional, the company more so.

As we stepped outside, we were drawn by the intoxicating smells of olive trees, pine, with the rich red earth cooling in the darkness.

The chirping of crickets was a continuous soft background tone beneath everything else, the sky ink-black, a perfect blanket of stars stretching from one horizon to the other. More stars than I could ever remember seeing back home. Our new adventure was well and truly alive and kicking; the days slowly slipping by too quickly.

I flinched as something flew out of the darkness, fluttering close to my head. The bats were out in force tonight.

The very atmosphere brought with it a feeling of instant intoxication.

Dozens of happy people were seated at trestle tables that ran down each side of the street.

Most of the time we spent in Lloret, we were in a state of euphoria, drinking and watching the world go by.

The old part of the town was full of moonlight and shadows, the pavements scrubbed scrupulously clean.

We felt alive as we rambled through the streets, under buildings with terracotta tiled roofs and blue wooden shutters, up steep steps, through archways.

A congregation of women was spilling from a church, while outside, beggars waited for any spare change. It was sad to see, but it was like that all the world over.

We came across a stag and hen party. The women were dressed in pink (pink to make the boys wink) drinking out of willy-shaped straws, while the men were dressed in various coloured Tutu's and matching leg warmers.

It was only harmless fun, and it made for a more memorable night.

As the days wore on, we all started to feel relaxed and at home. As we got closer to our van, the gap year lads invited us over to their van for a farewell drink, as they were moving on in the morning. You can't say no to that, can you?

We said we would be back in a few minutes with our chairs and drinks. And I have to say, there were a friendly bunch of lads.

Chapter Twenty-Five

A short while later, as we were sat, talking and drinking, I suddenly noticed Steve staring over towards something by the side of their van.

He quickly sat up, as though someone had pinched his bottom, then pointed out a large black mass, moving a few feet from one of the front wheels of the van, appearing to shift its shape.

We all stopped talking, transfixed on what we knew was an army of ants coming out of their nest, which at some point must have been disturbed.

Here we go again, recalling us having pitched one of our tents on one the last time we were here.

In a flash, one of the London guys ran into their van.

A few minutes later, he came out carrying a pan of boiling water, which he poured into the hole of the nest, resulting in thousands of ants scampering away.

Every part of the ground was a swirling mass of activity.

That hadn't worked as well as he'd imagined, so we all got up, stamping away like mad at them.

Some of them ran up Mikes legs, which he swiftly brushed away with his hands, at the same time jumping up and down as though he was walking on red hot sand.

He soon disappeared telling us that he was going for a quick shower.

Desperately trying to get this whole sorry incident over with, one of the other lads, dashed into the van, before returning with a can of lighter fuel and a box of matches.

Large angry ants were everywhere. Meanwhile, we had an audience of several inquisitive children along with their parents, who had told them to move a safe distance from the excitement.

Standing well back, he poured the contents of the fuel in the hole of the nest, then struck a match. Keeping his hand safely away from the fuel, he dropped the lighted match on the nest, which was swiftly followed by a small explosion of clumps of soil, grass, and ants, resembling a small volcano. We all just stood and stared, transfixed, remembering that we had done the same thing all those years ago.

It didn't completely kill all of the ants. What was left of them, vanished under the van. The guys then quickly moved their van a safe distance from what was left of the nest.

Talk about lightening striking twice. That pyrotechnic show brought the night to an enjoyable end.

We said our farewells to them, wishing them all the best, for the rest of their holiday, leaving the curious crowd to go back to their pitches, collecting our chairs and empty bottles, before gingerly making our way back to the van, keeping well away from any ants that might be lurking around, ready to take the destruction of their nest out on us.

There was no sign of any. It was now getting late; the camp site crowded with other groups.

After dark, the campfires grew rowdy with songs and lots of drink.

Chapter Twenty-Six

It was perfect sleeping weather, warm enough not to need my sleeping bag, yet warm enough to sleep in my boxer shorts.

After a long day, I was looking forward to a long night's sleep.

This particular night, Geoff decided to sleep in the tent with me, giving the others at bit more room to spread out, and to keep me company.

At some point through the night, there was a sound nearby that made my eyes pop open.

Normally, I can sleep through most everything – through thunderstorms or earthquakes.

In this case, it was something loud enough to wake me.

It was the sound of undergrowth being disturbed, followed by someone walking on the gravel path that ran by the side of the tent.

I sat bolt upright, the mental images of when we were on holiday together, when Steve was attacked during the night as we camped out at the side of a road, miles from nowhere.

The noise stopped for a few seconds, before a shadow passed in front of the tent, then stopping.

At that point, I asked Geoff if he was awake.

Thankfully, he was.

It was then when I told him that I thought someone was lurking outside the tent. Whatever it was, sounded large.

Geoff snored then told me to go back to sleep, reminding me that everything sounds louder at night.

That was true, but it didn't make me less frightened.

I gingerly slipped out of my sleeping bag, before shuffling on my knees to the foot of the tent.

At that point Geoff asked me what I was doing.

I quickly told him to be quiet, as I was going outside to investigate, because I wouldn't be able to sleep knowing there maybe someone outside, at the same time, hoping the others had locked the van.

Had I imagined it?

No! I heard it again.

Taking a deep breath, plucking up the courage, I cautiously unzipped the mesh, peering out.

It was pitch black. I couldn't see a thing.

Once my eyes had adjusted to the dark, I cautiously climbed out of the tent, searching for who'd made the noise.

I peered and peered, but for the life of me, I couldn't see anything, apart from the moon that brought enough light to see close by, along with the dim shapes of trees and bushes in the distance.

Eventually, I crawled back into the tent, pausing twice to check no one was hiding behind the tent, dreading seeing anyone.

I can tell you; it was a long time before I decided to get back in my sleeping bag for warmth and comfort.

I laid there staring at total darkness.

Eventually I fell asleep. In all the time I was outside, Geoff was snoring like a trooper. I'm getting too old for this!

There was no way I will be telling June the next time I called her.

I could hear her saying something like, *'I told you so. You never listen. And you can't be burning the candle at both ends at you age'*, blah, blah, blah . . .Z-z-z-z-z.

Spooked by nothing more than my vivid imagination, I decided not to say anything to the others, just in case they took the mickey out of me.

The next day started well enough, with a sunny dawn that promised another hot day, the experience from the night before just a distant memory.

By the time we finished having a wash, it was nine o'clock with the sun already high and blazing.

The rain had flattened the long grass like a stampeding herd of cattle.

The sun was out now and, as I poured myself a glass of orange juice, Nigel suggested the five of us go for a bike ride.

Chapter Twenty-Seven

Even on hot days, the woods where we were camped out were normally cool, which was a bonus.

Nevertheless, the air was heavy and listless and steamy, almost tropical, when I woke up.

After breakfast, which consisted of a selection of cereals and loads of coffee, we cleared everything away, then headed into town to find a shop that hired out bikes.

There was one on the site, but by this time, all of the bikes had been spoken for.

We had only walked a mile, before we came across one that had bikes that suited us.

Not too fancy yet looking as though they were well maintained.

After paying the owner, he warned us not to go too far as he'd heard that there was a thunderstorm heading our way.

Last time we hired bikes; Nigel got knocked down by a crazy French guy.

He wasn't injured, just bruised and a little shaken. He didn't need hospital treatment, so this time we were being extra vigilant.

We made our way cautiously out of town, wheeling our bikes past the clutter of dinghies, kayaks, surfboards, and dripping wetsuits. All of them were encrusted with sand and slung over every available space on the wooden rail, all the while, pointing out various shops and bars that was still in business after all these years, including the Revolution.

We'd only cycled a few yards when I heard someone shouting for me to watch out.

In a blink of an eye, someone clattered into me with their shoulder, causing me to fall to the ground, with me finishing up sprawled out on my back.

The bike came with me, slamming its full force into my ankle.

For a moment, I just lay there, head to one side, looking up at this guy.

Then I heard someone asking me if I was okay.

I don't know who it was. To be honest, apart from a bruised backside, I felt fine.

Then all sorts of emotions rushed through me; my heart was pounding, adrenalin pumping, worried that I'd broken something, spoiling the holiday.

I asked if somebody could please help me up.

The guy who'd collided with me was still stood there, arms by his sides, just gawping at me.

Geoff told me later on in the day that the man was texting on his phone, not looking where he was going.

Sadly, that's the way of the world today.

People (mostly the young one's) thinking it's safe to text as they cross a busy road, even though the green man is showing, rather than looking out for traffic. Mind you, they will have plenty of time to text and phone their family and friends when they are lying in bed in hospital, all battered and bruised.

Sorry, I'll step down from my soap box now.

Steve picked up the bike that was still lying on my leg. Somehow, I staggered to my feet.

As I did so, I realised I must have not only bruised by backside. I'd injured my ankle as well.

I hobbled over to a bench by the side of the road.

Steve in the meantime had put the bike on its stand, by the side of me.

My bottom was burning from the fall.

I could see that I'd grazed my ankle quiet badly.

After gingerly moving it about, I knew it was just a sprain, thank God.

Finally, the man who'd knocked me off the bike came over to me apologising, offering his hand, which I took.

He said he was sorry, adding that he should have been looking where he was going, before asking me if I wanted a lift to the hospital.

I told him I was fine, and I'll just sit for a while, imagining when I wake up in the morning, my ankle will have a massive bruise, wondering what my backside will look like.

Actually, it turned out to be nowhere as bad as I thought. Thank goodness for small mercies.

We carried on in a convoy heading towards the relative safety of the woods, where there was less chance of being knocked over.

It started well, the roads were sound, the tarmac good and before us the countryside in the distance was breath-taking.

Sunlight dappled the path from time to time, yet for the next few minutes it resembled a jungle of a place, reminding me of the landscape in *Jurassic Park*. The leaves seemed bigger than normal; the trees taller.

They say once you know how to ride a bike it doesn't leave you yet riding a bike in these conditions was like being on a very unsteady, unpredictable animal that bucked at the slightest tremble of the handlebars; even moving my head at the wrong time was enough to throw me off balance for a second.

Moments later we found ourselves on a path through the woods that ran so straight it might have been scored with a ruler.

The trees tracked identically past, interspersed with leafless oaks.

There was something dreamlike about it, away from the hustle and bustle of the town.

Even the leaden sky made the place look enchanting. It was so peaceful.

The sun was already up in the sky, bringing promise of another uncomfortable hot day. Better than the rain the man had predicted.

The air under the tall trees was stifling; the strong breeze gusting eddies of loose, dusty soil about the weed-strewn ground like small tornadoes, sending loose bales of tumbleweed rolling along the ground.

The path rambled through the woods, the grass yellow from the summer sun, then into a rugged path, carpeted with acorns, crunching under the tyres.

For the first time it occurred to me that the woods were beautifully peaceful.

A solitary bird sang high up in the canopy of the branches above our heads, leaves rustled in the breeze coming from the beach.

The path began to blend seamlessly into undergrowth, its surface resembling craters of moon, that were uncomfortable to both my sore backside and my eye. I persevered, as you do, when on holiday.

The air was clean, plus my ankle had finally stopped aching.

As the day wore on, we noticed a few rain clouds heading our way, followed by a spot of rain. By this time, we were well and truly in the heart of the woods.

There was sweat at the small of my back and under my arms. At least there was some semblance of shade here.

I huffed and puffed up the hills and freewheeled down them, the path cutting through several fields, carefully avoiding the many writhing and interlacing roots, the ground rising steadily.

The rain had only been light up to that point – little more than a drizzle once it made it through the maze of canopy shielding the forest floor, but the sky was dark above.

The ground was damp but not mud, except where a gap in the canopy had let rain in.

Everything was still, and far-away sounds seemed near and clear.

Steve and Nigel started showing off, trying their hand at doing a wheelie.

The ground was riddled with holes and small stones, resulting in them both nearly falling off their bikes.

Both of them somehow managed to keep their balance.

Their faces looked a bit ashen.

It gave us laugh at their expense.

Then as the man predicted, it started to rain, in buckets.

We carried riding in the rain, the water lying so deep that now and again we were losing traction, aquaplaning, throwing up mud in the air, covering our bare legs and shorts.

Whose idea was it to hire bikes?

Boy, did it rain.

In my 70+ years I've never ridden in anything like it, far worse than the rain the other night when the tent nearly flew away over the trees to France . . .

The air was thick with humidity, the storm to our south casting the area into deep shadows.

The storm clouds pushed up fast and would be overhead soon.

Riding in the rain was fine, it's just a matter of keeping your concentration at all times and keeping the pace up, slowing things down in your mind, making sure what you were doing was smooth.

Especially me, as I didn't want any more accidents today, thank you.

The path became even worse.

At times, the gaps on the path were more pond than pothole, so wide that we had no choice but to ride through them, the water reaching the bikes axles and washing over our feet. The rain was a pounding torrent that made a thick wall of noise as it struck the leaves on the trees around us and the ground at our feet.

We were properly soaked now. We may as well have jumped into the pool, there wasn't a bit of us that wasn't totally drenched.

Storm clouds covered the sun, the temperature dropping a few degrees as the wind grew stronger.

We came across a sign in the woods which we all thought was hilarious and frightening at the same time.

!WARNING!

Hikers; please take extra precautions and wear little noisy bells on clothing to give advance warning and avoid surprising the animals.

We also suggest carrying pepper spray in case of an encounter with a wild boar that live in the area.

Be vigilant for fresh boar activity and distinguish between normal feces and boar feces.

Smaller animals feces are smaller and contain lots of berries, while the wild boar shit has bells in it and smells like pepper. Happy hiking.

Some of the bends were sweeping, winding our way between trees that was giving us some respite from the pouring rain.

We hit a series of bends. Nigel took a corner with the bike with him nearly keeling over. He somehow managed to keep the bike upright by putting on the brakes.

I slowed down, as I'd had enough excitement for one today.

When we eventually made it through the woods, we found ourselves on the main road leading back to the town.

We then cycled back to the bike hire shop.

Minutes later, we pulled up outside the bike hire shop. My heart fit to burst from the workout.

I noticed that the streets were busy despite the rain.

As we headed back to the campsite feasting on a takeaway McDonalds we were laughing and joking, at my expense I must say, about the events of the day that seemed as though it had happened a million years ago, and to someone else entirely.

That was until I felt a twinge in my ankle, along with a slight burning sensation in my Derry Air.

Meanwhile, the wind was getting slightly out of hand, spinning metal rotary signs outside petrol stations into a deafening turbine frenzy, as we passed on the way, sending waiters in pursuit of airborne parasols.

What a day this turned out to be. Mercifully, it had stopped raining, the air much cooler. When I spoke to June later on in the evening, I just told her we'd hired a bike for the day, and we got caught in the rain. She replied by saying, and sniggering may I add, 'It was reported on the news that yesterday had been one of the hottest day in the UK for months'. Touché. I never believe what they say on the news.

It was now just before 9 o'clock in the evening, drinking by the van, listening to the music from the 60's, talking for well over three hours.

There is nothing like a barbecue to incite one-upmanship between Brits on holiday.

Geoff went about it in the same way if he were at home, busying himself by loading the charcoal practically piece by piece, and not allowing one of us anywhere near.

He was clearly an expert, though.

Finally, he started cooking.

He seemed to have hands for tongs, like a hard-case Edward Scissorhands.

The air had a golden quality, the evening light soft and honey warm as the sun slowly sunk toward the hills in the distance.

All about us were French families, smiling and enjoying their evening meals, their table heaving with barbecued fish, quiches, salads, and bottles of red wine.

For a change, we said we would call into one of the sport's bars the following day. It would soon be the longest day of the year.

All but one of us were happy; Nigel pulled a face. He wasn't into football, more of a rugby league kind of guy.

He said he would grin and bear it, not wanting to be a party pooper. We also reminded him that our pub crawling days were well and truly over, leaving it the young ones who could while away the night, like we did all those years ago.

What great memories . . .

By midnight, the toll of cycling was getting to us, along with the several night-caps, so we decided to call it a night.

To be honest, I can't understand how they like the stuff, in fact, they all taste the same to me.

But I went along with them, finishing off with a bottle of lager, hoping to take the fiery taste away of the whisky.

Before I go any further, there will be instances in the narrative when there wasn't much to report.

For instance, just sitting by the van, emptying the waste, cleaning out the van, talking, telling jokes, lazing about during the day by the van, reading, listening to music on my Amazon Echo, or uneventful days soaking up the sun on the beach. Sampling the various whisky's, they'd brought along with them at night.

There were also certain mornings when I woke up not knowing what day it was, and other days where I didn't write anything down due to them merging into one. That said, I'm pretty sure you will get an idea of what happened to the five of us over the two weeks from what's been said so far.

Chapter Twenty-Eight

The following morning my head was thumping, my limbs aching, especially my ankle, as if I'd run a marathon instead of riding a bike for a few hours.

I was lying face down, still wearing my clothes. I opened my eyes a crack.

Due to our late night, again, none of us stirred until 10 a.m. When we eventually woke up, we decided to spend the afternoon down by the beach.

It was another fine day, a warm sun that was bright and distinct, burning the morning mist, leaving the sky a cloudless robin's-egg blue.

While the others prepared breakfast, consisting of cereal and coffee, I rubbed some magic cream on my backside in the van, as I didn't want to be arrested for flashing.

Thankfully my ankle hadn't swollen, it just felt tender. It didn't stop me from walking.

Before making our way to the beach, we wandered through the centre of town, towards the market, to do a bit of shopping. I love foreign markets. I love the look and smell, plus the glorious unfamiliarity of them.

By the time we arrived, the place was lively, with tons of great stalls selling fresh food, souvenirs, and several other items too many to mention. I particularly enjoyed the variety of typical foods, Spanish hams, cheeses, besides the ambience of the market.

It was surrounded by restaurants and shops, so it made for a very nice area of the town.

I narrowed my eyes, looking into the distance.

The market was crowded and packed with stalls under brightly striped awnings which stretched right to the end of the long, gravel square, where, I would assume, on quieter days, old men played boules, chewing the fat in the sun.

Every local Spanish housewife worth her salt was here; the whole place positively bristled with them.

They sniffed and prodded the abundant displays of brightly coloured peppers, vibrant green courgettes, often dismissing them and certainly bartering energetically, before they designed to make a purchase.

If customers in the UK did that, they'd have their hands chopped off by the stall holder.

Minutes later, we stopped for a coffee in a shady part of the town.

The only other customers were a couple of old men with their walking sticks propped up against the table beside them.

The Spanish flag hung listlessly from the town hall next to the café, no breeze at all to stir it in the early morning heat.

There was an abundance of stalls selling fresh meat, fish, vegetables, herbs, etc. It was a feast for the eyes.

A small pack of mixed-bred cats of different sizes lounged close to the fish stalls, begging for scraps, yet keeping a safe distance from the stall-holders who were scaring them away with their enormous fish knives, only for the cats to return once the stall-holders backs were turned.

There was other places you could enjoy coffee, tea, wine etc at one of the many bars lining the road, with super friendly people. Tables and chairs were provided, making it a perfect setting for a relaxed afternoon.

We strolled through the stalls, discovering local pastries and savoury snacks, where you can sit and relax with a craft beer or a glass of wine and listen to live music.

The atmosphere was relaxing and cheerful. I love wandering around foreign markets. At their best, or to be frank, even at their most mediocre, they are enough to make a British tourist weep with frustration at the pathetic fare we have to offer and served in the UK. Where the fruit and veg stall, stands between a stall selling knock-off batteries, with another offering ten pairs of socks for a fiver.

Any of the half-dozen fish counters in this particular market were 100 times more impressive than any fishmonger's spread in Britain, knowing how fresh it all is not least because most of it is still twitching.

Half an hour later, we were heading for the beach, sampling a few of the tantalising food items on offer.

It would have been the perfect place to spend an afternoon going from stall to stall, tasting the various dishes and drinks, but we had planned for the rest of the day down on the beach.

We bought soft ice creams from one of the stalls, before winding our way slowly to the beach, passing a number of African guys, relentlessly and unsuccessfully trying to sell us watches, hats, balls, sunglasses, and even fake Gucci handbags, along with small carved elephants.

We didn't bother, pretending we couldn't understand what they were saying.

You will have to bear with me for a moment for the next bit, as I can't stop laughing, thinking about what I have to write.

Like Geoff, Steve is a dog lover, in fact Steve has two Labradoodles.

Anyhow, as we were slowly making our way to the beach, I saw in the distance, what I can only characterize, as a young lady, being dragged along the promenade by four Labradoodles.

She had what I could only describe as having a large chest, bursting from all sides, out of her skimpy T-shirt.

As we drew closer to her, Steve came out with, 'I bet those two are a handful to control'.

The woman stopped dead in her tracks, followed by an awkward silence.

At first, the five of us hadn't realised what he'd said, until the girl stopped, giving Steve a filthy look.

The moment Steve had blurted out the words, I could see that he could have bitten his tongue. After that, we kept on laughing all the way to the beach. Can you blame us? What a corker of a comment from Steve.

By this time, the Mediterranean was glittering so much, it was as if someone had thrown the world's supply of diamonds across a floor of sapphire-coloured marble. Small waves whipped up by a gentle offshore breeze bringing a note of coolness to the merciless midday sunshine.

Our intrepid little group was subdued after last night, our beach towels grouped around a backpack, and books.

The smell of suntan lotion mingled with a salty breeze off the sea, mixed with cigarette smoke that drifted over from a French couple nearby.

The couple didn't smoke for too long because a policeman came over ordering them to put them out, reminding them that smoking was forbidden on the beach.

Even at my age, I can honestly describe myself as still being a 'dedicated follower of fashion'. Even as far back as my late teens.

But as far as having a tattoo, body piercing and diamond stud earrings are concerned, well, that's definitely out of the question.

The reason why I've mentioned it, is because there was a group of what looked like six middle-aged men lazing about a few feet away from us.

All six had tattoos of some kind of another, adorning their bodies. In fact, one of them had a shaved head, which was completely covered in them, and most of his neck.

Well, if you run out of reading matter, while relaxing on the beach, you can always go across and check out the intricate designs of dragons, swirls, football club motifs, and God knows what else.

What I cannot understand; do they have any idea what they will look like when they are in their seventies.

Unfortunately, in this day and age, I don't think it matters anymore.

And don't get me started on man buns, especially the ones that look like a waterspout coming out of the top of their heads, or the ones that look like a dog turd.

We have to accept it. Doesn't mean we have to like it.

Come to think of it, maybe I should change the title of the book to Four Old *'Gits'* and One grumpy Old *'Git'* ...

It was now late in the afternoon on what had so far already been an extremely long day, so we decided to go back to the van to freshen up before going out for the night.

While Mike was getting himself ready for the evening, I noticed that he had brought enough aftershaves for a soccer team to prepare for a night on the town.

After we had all sampled a few, the inside of the van smelled like the fragrance section at the duty free.

Tonight, we were going to go to the Gotham for a change, and to see if it had changed.

It did, in fact none of us recognised the place, which on the face of it, we wouldn't expect it to be after all these years.

The atmosphere in the Gotham was electric.

There was all kind of good music to suit everyone's taste, even us. Moreover, the DJ was on fire (not literally).

Steve went across to the DJ, requesting him to play a song, which brought back more memories. It was, *Honky Tonk Woman* by the Rolling Stones.

The five of us just stood by the edge of the dancehall, singing away to ourselves, grinning ...

All the staff were friendly with us old folks, but we did stand out, which we knew we would. Our money was as good as anybody's, so we enjoyed ourselves for an hour.

No beer is ever as large as the one you mime with your hands when requesting a lager on holiday, or the indignity of realising you can't really handle carrying five pints at once when only halfway back to your table. Somehow, I managed.

For a complete change from the norm, we decided to visit Waterworld which was just outside of town the following day.

As we slowly made our way to the camp site, we could hear music and laughter coming from the centre of town.

It sounded as though there was some kind of festival going on, which we weren't aware of.

It wasn't until we noticed the coloured flyers pinned on the trees, fluttering in the breeze, that there was a late night shopping event, taking place in the centre of Lloret this evening.

Not only were the shops open until 12.00 midnight - 12.30ish but there was live music, shows, food, DJ's, drag shows and lots more, all located in the squares and streets around the church.

We were too tired to visit any of the shows, including the drag shows, but we were surprised to see three drag artists venture into the night from one of the bars, along with two stunning woman, with legs right up to their necks.

All of them were covered from head to toe in brightly coloured feathers and glittering sequins. For a brief moment, we'd lost sight of Nigel. That was when we spotted him chatting to one of the women. Or what Nigel thought were women.

Mike casually stepped up to Nigel and whispered in his ear, informing Nigel they were men.

You should have seen the look on Nigel's face. The silence was deafening.

No!

Yes!

You should have gone to Spec-Savers Nigel.

Well, at least the night finished on a high note. That was until the lady-boy spoke in a low note.

Nigel saw the funny side of it, as we all fell about laughing. His excuse was that he'd had a skin-full that night. We all did.

Chapter Twenty-Nine

None of us wanted to drive to Waterworld the next day, so we took the free shuttle bus in the morning from Lloret.

On the off chance we may at some point during the holiday have to wear face masks, I'd packed a few in my backpack, with my swimming trunks, towel, and sun lotion, which came in handy, as we had to wear them on the bus taking us to and from Waterworld.

After a short bus ride, the bus was soon pulling up in the car park by the reception.

To our surprise, it was only 30 euros admission for the day.

Since the age of four, I'd been wearing glasses.

In 2019, I had my cataracts removed, and for the first time in over sixty years I could see clearly without them.

I still have to wear them for reading and close up, so that meant I didn't have to worry about anyone knocking my glasses off or getting wet, as I wasn't going to wear them today when in the water.

As for the others, they said it was weird seeing me without glasses.

I was well out of my comfort zone, as I wasn't the best of swimmers, only good enough to save my life.

I took it in my stride, not regretting it in the slightest.

The park was on the edge of Lloret and in the middle of a pine forest. It boasted over 20 attractions.

All we were interested in, was to chill out in one of the large swimming pools and going on the white-knuckle water slides.

For the adrenalin seekers in the group, going on one of the spectacular, high speed slides or the white water courses, where you could let yourselves be carried away on the 2 meter high waves in the wave pool or race down a snaking tube with a rubber boat or tyre from the slide.

I was reluctant at first, then after seeing Nigel, Steve and Mike have a go, I took the plunge, along with Geoff as he was also reluctant.

All I can say it was amazing. Just like being a ten year old all over again. An adrenalin rush to end all adrenalin rushes.

Boy was it good.

Because I'd been sat in the sun for over an hour, the water in the main pool was ice cold, brutal, paralysing cold. It felt like frozen fire, a million tiny needles piercing my skin all at once.

After an hour, I'd had enough, so I headed over to a shaded part to dry off, watching the silly antics of four old men playing the fool, which brough a huge smile to my face.

In addition to endless attractions, there were several restaurants and kiosks on the site, where you could get refreshments such as fries, burgers, ice cream, chips, snacks, or drinks.

By late afternoon, we were shattered and famished, so we dried ourselves off, changed into our dry clothes, placing our trunks and T-shirts in a plastic bag, before putting them in one of the backpacks we'd brought with us, then headed over to one of the kiosks selling burgers and fries.

I was so hungry I could have eaten a scabby horse.

It was getting late in the afternoon by now. In a few more hours the day would be ebbing away, also by the looks of it, most of the other holiday makers had packed up and left.

By this time, we'd had enough, so we caught the bus back to town.

Chapter Thirty

It was still hot when we got back to the campsite, so we sat by the side of the swimming pool, relaxing for an hour.

Mike went back to the van, returning a few minutes later, balancing a few plates, along with a choice of bread, cheese, plus a selection of fruit, which we really enjoyed, which was nice thought, and making a change to what we'd been eating.

The area was filled with parents with young children, all screaming and splashing each other.

Teenage boys wore garish long trunks, the girls in tiny bikinis, all plugged into their iPods, sunglasses on, a paperback apiece.

Oh, to be young and free and single again.

A group of girls over on the other side of the pool were screaming and laughing as they took it in turns to be thrown into the pool by a couple of lads, all taking selfies on their mobile phones.

That didn't last long, as one of the staff came out, pointing to a sign, which showed them that diving and throwing other people was against the rules.

We left the swimming pool after an hour, having persisted long enough with the noise of the young children, who were either bored or hungry, or both. As we were nearing the end of the holiday, we decided to treat ourselves, by booking a table at the Al Freskito restaurant, that we'd stumbled upon while walking on the promenade the other day.

The light changed as the afternoon slipped into evening. Crickets filled the evening air with their soft burr as we meandered slowly down the hill to the restaurant.

There were a number of restaurants close by that offered a two-course meal for ten euros a head, ours was a grander affair, catering for the posher end of the market with an obligatory five course menu.

Al Freskito restaurant

We weren't disappointed. The service was first class, the food delicious.

We all had the 5 course meal with fresh local produce, and a bottle of wine, all for €16.

It takes experience to canter through a five-course *a la carte* menu complete with *paella,* not to mention a strong cup of coffee. We all had years of it. These days, to travel overseas and not embrace the local eating culture seems to me downright irresponsible.

As we ordered a second round of beers, a couple of old guys carrying acoustic guitars emerged through from the inside of the restaurant and began playing a batch of songs.

The bar staff and waiters joined in, singing along, along with the locals on the other tables who seemed to know it well.

Within a few moments virtually all the customers started clapping and singing in unison, we did, even though we didn't know the words.

It didn't matter as our voices were being drowned out by the others, as we soaked up the atmosphere.

What a great end to the evening and the holiday in Lloret.

Just before we'd settled the bill, one of the waiters appeared from behind the beaded curtain, balancing a cake with a single candle on, quickly followed by a rendition of Happy Birthday from the other four. Bastards.

I thought they'd forgotten about my 73rd birthday.

Anyway, it was a nice surprise.

Even the other diners sang along.

After they had finished singing, I stood up, before taking a bow, then doffing an imaginary hat.

After all that, my birthday was the following day the 23rd June, which they all knew. But because it was the day before we were due to leave, we had decided that none of us would drink any alcohol that night, also we hadn't made any plans to go out, so according to Steve, that was the reason they brought the cake out that night.

I have to say, it did bring a tear to my eyes, knowing that they had remembered. I found out later from Geoff; Steve nipped into town to buy the cake while I was having a shower. And he'd already had the candle in the van.

Then I remembered him coming back to the van, looking sheepishly, saying he'd done some last minute shopping, buying a few fridge magnets for his wife, Jean. If I said she had a few fridge magnets, it would be an understatement – she had hundreds of them.

We paid the bill, leaving a generous tip, then slowly made our way towards the start of the coastal path that passes through Lloret de Mar, which runs down the entire Catalan coastline, showcasing its coves, beaches, and landscapes. The sun hovering above the calm shimmer of the sea.

Bathing in the neon glow of the bars and clubs, soaking up the atmosphere, we found ourselves jostling with several rowdy youths, all shouting at the top of their voices, as they watched a re-run of one of the Nations Cup match's; while we were breathing in the hot fat smells of a hundred and one takeaway meals, forcing ourselves to endure the constant thump of countless anonymous club tracks, which as far as I am concerned all sounded the same. Well, nothing's changed. As we had only one more day in Lloret, we sat and talked for a while, congratulating each other, having managed, so far, to do what we had set out to do.

Oh, and drinking what was left of the whisky. I had a couple of glasses, which burned the back of my throat.

Sorry guys, I'll stick to lager, thank you very much.

Chapter Thirty-One

Just one more full day before having to leave Lloret, so we decided to do some last minute shopping after breakfast.

June sent me a funny birthday message on her phone, but I couldn't possibly tell you what it said. LOL.

By the time we reached the market, it was heaving with shoppers, all bartering with stall holders.

I was surprised to see that most of the people were not wearing a face mask.

Apart from its vibrant nightlife, beautiful beaches, and countless activities, Lloret has a large traditional weekly market where you can buy the best souvenirs, at the best prices.

That's where we spent the rest of the day, soaking up the atmosphere, tasting some of the food on offer.

There's nothing like sniffing around for that real bargain.

We walked past a number of stalls selling everything from artisan cheese, sarongs, and second-hand books, none of them English. The aroma of pasties competed with the scent of handmade soaps. Most of the people were milling around the stalls, mostly drawn to the food like bees around a honey jar.

One area was given over to traditional fairground attractions with a wooden helter-skelter towering over the area. The children were making a beeline for it.

June told me in no uncertain terms not to bring back anything tatty, such as a flamenco dancer or a stuffed toy bull with a spear stuck in its neck, only some cigarettes from the duty free on my way home.

I did buy them for Mark and Caroline, along with an annoying pair of clicking castanets, as a housewarming gift as a joke, knowing after we'd left their house, they'd all end up in the dustbin.

At first, I had to haggle with the man in the shop, until I walked away, before he called me back. I did buy them a bottle of caramel liquor which I know they liked.

I couple of us called into a gift shop that was filled with your standard tourist items; Spanish lace, little dolls in flamenco costumes, T-shirts with slogans even students would be embarrassed to wear. Cigarette lighters of every, shape, colour and size, and numerous plates with scenes of Spain, besides other cheap rubbish you see all over the world, the lot. Oh, and would you believe it, glow-in-the-dark-condoms. Considering it was our last day in Lloret, we were all in good spirits. I just think we now wanted to get home. To be honest, I did. I don't know about the others. I kept that to myself.

After strolling around the market, searching for that final gift in the shops in the town, with the afternoon turning to evening, we slowly headed off back to the campsite to pack.

Dusk was now upon us. Dark shadows pooled in the streets under the lights from the bars and restaurants, softening the edges of the buildings.

My mood was now fluctuating between excitement about seeing June, Mark, Caroline, and my grandsons, yet on the other hand, I had pangs of sadness that we'd never get another chance of the five of us being together like this again.

Life as they say, goes on.

As agreed, no alcohol was consumed that evening, so we spent a couple of hours packing and cleaning the van, taking any food that was left to the waste bins.

Chapter Thirty-Two

Friday morning, the last day of our holiday was a flurry of activity.

While we were packing up, Steve checked the tyres. He'd already filled the tank the day before.

Barcelona here we come. By the Sat-Nav, it was just two hours away, so we should arrive around before noon.

Why is it when you are on holiday, the first week goes by slowly, yet the last week flies by.

Before leaving, we sent texts home, reminding them that we were going to visit Barcelona for a couple of hours before setting off back, and with a following wind, hoping to arrive back in Bradford sometime Saturday afternoon.

We knew that going to Barcelona was out of our way.

We'd already agreed we wouldn't visit Paris or London this time round, as we'd already been there before as a group.

Once we cleared the pitch of any litter, ensuring everything was carefully stored away in their respective compartments in the van, we said goodbye to Lloret and drove onto Barcelona.

Barcelona, the cosmopolitan capital of Spain's Catalonia region, is known for its arts and architecture. The fantastical Sagrada Familia church and other modernist landmarks designed by Antoni Gaudi dot the city. Museu Picasso and Fundació Joan Miro feature modern art by their namesakes. City history museum MUHBA, includes several Roman archaeological sites.

Gradually the green landscape gave way to mile after mile of car showrooms, glass-fronted office complexes and ugly new-build high-rise flats, that probably would probably cost you an arm and a leg to buy.

The problem we now had, was finding a large enough car park for the Motorhome. We needn't have worried as we soon found one and walking distance from the centre.

By this time, the morning sun was already shining in between the leaves of the ancient trees lining the walkways, shadows playing on peoples upturned faces; taking in the beautiful buildings, while soaking up the atmosphere.

To our astonishment and relief, we noticed that there was no shortage of car parks for Motorhomes.

Avenues were packed with cafes, restaurants, souvenir shops, food, drink kiosks, all mixed with flower stalls, their fragrances floating in the morning air. We continued on, passing beautiful eighteenth-century buildings with ornamented windows and elaborate iron work on the balcony railings.

Chapter Thirty-Three

We soon set off towards *La Rambla,* where spray-painted human statues stood motionless among the passing crowds, and buskers, crooning crowd-pleasing classics, along with round-the-clock stalls that sold everything.

Moments later, we were making our way through the warren of narrow cobbled-stone streets, finding ourselves in the central district, before walking past numerous crowded cafes with outdoor tables, fruit and vegetable markets overflowing with local produce and sweet-smelling flowers.

On the way to *La Rambla,* we stopped by the side of the park watching a number of street artists perform mimes, jugglers and magicians, unicyclists, musicians, and dancers.

We just stood there in awe, watching them all.

Then a person dressed as a Greek statue suddenly moved forward plucking a coin from behind a young child's ear.

The child screamed, holding her hand up to her mouth.

She didn't run away.

Then to everyone's amazement, the statue opened his hand, before handing over the coin to girl. She took it, smiling.

The statue then smiled back giving her an official salute, causing the onlookers to clap and cheer.

As we carried on walking down the road, we came upon a man standing in a static pose, with his jacket, tie, and hair, fixed in a windy style.

It was my nephew, Wayne Scott, my sister's youngest son.

He quickly noticed us. He put on a show for us, by beginning to parody the audience.

Then to everyone's alarm, he hugged an old woman who was stood watching, before clowning about, much to the delight of us all, the old women thinking it was very funny.

"That's the famous *Windy Man*, children," I heard someone call out

Once Wayne had finished his routine, we stood for a few minutes talking to him. It had been awhile since I'd seen him.

Wayne was also Geoff's nephew. I won't go into that. Oh! Go on I will and see if you can work it out.

My sisters, husband (now divorced) brother's wife's, sister's husband is ME! Did you manage to work it out?

Or another way. My wife's sisters husbands brothers wife's brother is me. I've made it easier for you by taking out 'now divorced'.

Wayne told us he'd been living in Barcelona off and on for several years.

The last time I'd seen him, was when I came across him in Leicester Square in London.

After wishing him well, we slowly made our way into the centre.

Over the course of the next fifteen minutes, we came across a Gold Cowboy, who had lasso and a gun, posing for photos, wiggling his hips whilst shooting his fake pistol and swinging his lasso, much to the delight of the many tourists, especially young boys.

By this time, we were getting bored, so we headed over to the pier.

Hills tumbled down to the water's edge, sunlight washing across the marina, the bay hugging the town, along with the lights from the exquisite hotels lining the harbour, dancing on the rippling waters.

The bustling waterfront was swarming with passengers, food and luggage transport, plus other commercial vehicles, bringing fuel and cargo into the port, along with a large cruise ship that was moored along the waterfront.

Extravagant yachts bobbed up and down from the incoming tide in the harbour. Far away in the distance; elegant villas nestled on the hillside.

All along the dockside railings, passengers waved goodbye, taking pictures on their phones, all sharing the moment with the other guests around them, before the grand ship sailed slowly from its moorings, while dozens of seabirds dove into the waves.

The sun was to our backs, reflecting in the waters. Everything shone and glistened like the surface of a mirror.

The sky had taken on a faint pinkish tinge at the edges, which was reflected in the water, the windows of the buildings lining the port, along with the salty smell of salt borne on the wind.

Making our way down the marina, we heard a commotion, with what sounded like tables and chairs being thrown about.

As we got closer to where the noise was coming from, we spotted a couple of waiters frantically shooing away with their tea towels, three seagulls the size of puppies. The gulls were fighting each other over small scraps of food that had been left on the tables by the last diners.

The seagulls soon got the better of the waiters, as they didn't want their eyes plucking out.

At one point when we were heading to the famous *Sagrada Familia*, Mike was swept away by a tidal wave of Japanese tourists, all wearing cameras the size of microwaves, strapped around their necks.

Due to his *'Where's Wally'* red and white T-shirt, he stood out like a sore thumb.

After the rest of us had jumped up and down, waving our hands in the air, shouting like rowdy football fans, he safely made his way back to us.

Nothing prepares you at first for the impact of *Sagrada Familia,* as we gazed up at the impressive structure.

The whole area around the church was buzzing with activity: men dangled from spires, along with several stone masons carving huge slabs of stone, with cranes and scaffolding littering the vast, spectacular site.

We all stood in awe, observing the final construction that was in progress, trying to grasp the monumental scale of the project.

You may be interested to know; the church was only partially complete when *Gaudi* died in 1926.

As a work in progress, it offers the unique chance to watch the eighth wonder of the world in the making.

During the last 80 years, at incalculable cost may I add, sculptors and architects have added their own touches to *Gaudi's* dream, which is now financed by over a million visitors each year.

It's estimated that the project will be complete by 2026, the 100th anniversary of *Gaudi's* death."

Seeing as we were in Barcelona, having a couple of hours to spare, Steve, Geoff and Mike said that they would like to take the opportunity of visiting the Camp Nou stadium, the home of FC Barcelona, if it was at all possible.

Nigel and I weren't all that bothered going, as we weren't into football like the others, so we agreed to meet up in an hour.

The three of them set off towards the stadium, while we strolled around the area, before finding a cosy coffee bar, where we could sit and watch the world go by, and where the others would see us on their return.

Camp Nou was built between 1954 and 1957 and was officially opened on the September 24th, 1957, with a football match between FC Barcelona and a selection of players from the city of Warsaw.

The stadium replaced Barcelona's previous ground Camp de les Corts, which though could hold 60,000 spectators, was still too small for the growing support of the club.

Camp Nou initially consisted of two tiers that could hold 93,000 spectators.

The club has also what is considered to be the best football museum in the world, receiving more visitors than any other museum in Catalonia.

Exhibits trace the history of the club since it was founded more than century ago, while the guided tour takes you through the tunnel and into the changing rooms.

We'd only been sitting for a few minutes, when this guy came across, asking if we had any spare change. We both said no, before we carried on drinking our coffee.

I'd already spotted a couple of beggars a few minutes ago, one of which I would call being abusive as he started shouting as a young girl passed him without acknowledging him.

Then another guy stepped towards us, this time demanding we handed over some money.

One of his dirt encrusted hands was thrust out at us, in a threatening manner.

I think because we looked old, we would be easy pickings.

He was in for a surprise.

Over the years I'd become hardened. I was used to being bullied, and I wasn't going to be threatened, fleeced, or roughed up by a smelly yob.

I nodded over at Nigel, before we both swiftly got to our feet, stepping closer to him.

Standing at six foot four, weighing in at 16 stone, it can be quite intimidating for someone at five feet nothing.

That being the case, he took a step back, which we were grateful for, because the stench coming from him was making my eyes water.

Nevertheless, we needn't have worried, as two of the waiters suddenly appeared from café, telling him in no uncertain terms in Spanish to sling his hook, which Nigel nor myself could understand.

Suddenly the tables had turned. The down-and-out clearly understood what had been said, resulting in him walking away, no doubt cursing us under his breath.

As we are all aware, begging is becoming a widespread issue that every country in the world including the richest nations on the globe have their own share of beggars.

It can be off-putting, walking past beggars, mostly men, lying in shop doorways at night, wrapped in filthy blankets.

Yes, it's sad. They have to go somewhere. It makes the atmosphere a little scary, which puts people off going to places, such as Barcelona. Even some of the advanced nations in the world including the United States of America and the United Kingdom have beggars in one form or the other while mostly commonly beggars can be easily sighted in the third world countries.

Just as we'd finished out second cup of coffee, thinking that the three of them were here for the rest of the holiday, I spotted them heading our way, all three grinning like Cheshire cats.

For the next hour, as we made our way back to the van, they were waxing lyrical, continually rabbiting on about what they had seen. The main building where they visited the Trophy room, the museum, dressing rooms, the press conference room, and the stands.

Nigel and I just hummed and harred, nodding our heads. They were happy, and we were happy to let them carry on.

We wandered around the streets a little longer, soaking up the atmosphere, before deciding we'd had enough, then walking back to the van, which was a short distance away.

Chapter Thirty-Four

Once we were nicely settled in our seats and buckled up, we drove out of the car park, before starting the last leg of what had been another memorable holiday.

The satnav was showing us that we had at least fourteen hours of driving before reaching our last port of call, Calais, then driving North, and home . . .

I spent my time wisely, as I watched the world pass us by through the van's window, jotting down all the things that we'd done over the last two weeks in my logbook.

Occasionally, I would nod off, only for me to recall something else that I'd forgotten, which I quickly wrote down. I was just hoping I would be able to read my writing when putting this book together.

To be honest at the time, while I was putting pen to paper, it pained me, knowing that this would be our last overseas holiday together.

The following hours went with a blur and getting some serious milage under our belt. Thankfully, we had no problems crossing the Pyrenees, in fact it was less stressful as I thought.

Before I knew it, we were driving on the motorway towards Rouen . . .

I could have written; the drive was going smoothly. That was until we reached the outskirts of Rouen as the afternoon turned to evening.

211

The motorway from Rouen to Calais was virtually traffic free, which suited me down to the ground, as I was getting bored.

At this rate, I thought we'd get to the ferry port in plenty of time to catch the ferry.

While I was thinking that, wondering what time we'd get home, my thoughts were suddenly broken by the sudden appearance in the side view mirror of the first car I'd seen in ages, hurtling towards us from behind, dust and exhaust fumes rising.

It seemed to have appeared out of nowhere.

For the first few minutes, everything seemed normal.

Moments later, I was sure we were touching bumper to bumper, as I couldn't see any signs of the car. I didn't feel any kind of impact or a shunt, thank God.

I made the others aware. Steve said not to worry, asking us to keep an eye on the car, as they would soon pass us.

That didn't happen.

Steve toed the gas hoping to lengthen the gap.

In a flash I saw the drivers face in the side view mirror, along with a man in the passenger side and what looked like two more passengers sat in the back.

They stayed close behind us for several yards, before the car tried to overtake us, straddling the white line in the middle of the road, then pulling alongside.

Then all of a sudden, the brake lights flared, letting us pass on the inside, before the car pulled in once again behind us.

While Steve was concentrating on his driving, I kept glancing fearfully back, wondering what the driver was going to do next.

For a few seconds I lost sight of the car, before the idiot driver passed us on the right hand side, on the hard shoulder, resulting in dust and small stones rising from the ground.

Steve yanked the wheel to the left to avoid crashing straight into the back of the car.

Tyres smoked and screeched. Steve called out for us to grab hold of something.

In the meantime, I could clearly see the driver of the car fighting the wheel.

The car left a cloud of brake dust, tyre smoke and exhaust fumes, leaving criss-crossing lines of burnt rubber on the road surface behind it.

For a second it looked as though the driver might keep the car on the hard shoulder, but it was only a brief moment of calm before he lost control.

The vehicle ended up driving on the grass, missing a line of trees by inches before the driver eventually managed to get the car back on the hard surface, the car veering left, almost tipping onto two wheels, before the driver got the car back on a straight line.

In the smoky haze, I caught a glance of the car speeding off into the distance. I have to admit at the time, I was bricking it.

What the . . .! An illegal overtake.

Who cared, all I wanted was for us all to get home in one piece.

That was the moment when I began to realise that the car's driver wasn't just some drunken idiot with no respect for the rules of the road. He knew exactly what he was doing.

During our family holidays, I'd become aware of unsuspecting motorists being targeted in France, with tourists having often been singled out as easy targets because of the foreign number plates, and a GB sticker.

Motorists were warned when driving around France, that the scammer would convince the innocent driver that they had damaged a side view mirror of the scammer's car.

The scammer would then persuade the driver to pay damages right there on the spot instead of going through an insurance company.

Another popular trick I'd heard is the fake breakdown when the scammer flags a car down on the pretence of needing assistance while an accomplice slips into your car, grabbing whatever they can.

This is what I thought was happening to us.

My hands were shaking as I gripped the seat.

We all agreed that we should stop at the next rest area, to calm our nerves. I was now beginning to think they'd gone for good.

Chapter Thirty-Five

We never got to the rest area. About a mile down the motorway, we spotted the car, parked by the side of the road in one of the many rest areas.

We suggested to Steve that he should pull over as well, which he did, but not too close.

From where we stopped, we could make out four figures, leaning against their car, smoking.

For the time being we were going nowhere.

It was now what you could call a Mexican standoff.

We certainly wasn't going to move, and by the looks of their faces and the way they stood, they weren't.

Suddenly my heart was beating like it was fighting for space.

I thought our holiday was meant to be *fun*.

Ten minutes later, to our relief, the four men got back in their car and drove off in a cloud of dust, leaving the five of us alone.

We waited another ten minutes before we set off, at slower pace as we had no intentions of catching them up.

Much to my relief and probably, if I was honest, for the sake of a change of underwear, I'm glad we didn't come to blows with the four men.

As we were passing a service station, hoping we were out of danger, the car pulled out of the slip road from the right, then squeezed themselves in a small gap just feet in front of us.

We'd been too distracted to see it until the last moment.

Shit! I thought we'd seen the last of them.

Steve told us to make sure we were all wearing our seatbelts, because the next few minutes may get hairy.

That was the last thing I wanted.

We carried on regardless, hoping they were getting fed up, playing silly buggers. I was wrong.

Steve was saying nothing, just concentrating on his driving, the gap narrowing.

A mile down the road the driver hit his brakes. Steve slammed on his brakes, the van swerving to the left, before he pulled the wheel to the right to compensate, resulting in the van skidding to a stop on the hard shoulder.

I caught sight of Steve's eyes in the rear-view mirror: they were narrowed in grim determination as he tried to slow down the van.

My head whipped forward so fast that my glasses flew off the end of my nose.

Luckily I caught them before they landed on the floor, before grabbing the edge of the seat. At the same time, like the others, the seatbelts dug into our chests.

Steve had had a fair idea what the driver intended doing, so he was one step ahead. We didn't ram into the back of car, which was their intentions.

Steve's earlier advice came to mind before we left Geoff's house, when he said not to leave anything lying about that could roll on the floor, or in this case fly towards us from the back of the van.

Even so, if those guys thought they could intimidate five old gits, they had another thing coming.

We had all come across bully's before. This time we weren't going to let them get one over us and intimidate us.

Now this is when it got a bit nervy.

The four guys jumped out of the car, then cockily stood at the rear of their car.

They had probably rehearsed this part many times in their macho fantasies, none of which could possibly prepare them for what we had in store for them.

We just hoped *they* weren't armed to the teeth.

The leader of the group looked obvious, as I'd seen the likes of them in many a movie.

He was the tallest of the four, and most likely the oldest, and definitely not as old as us five.

He had long, greasy hair that hung straight down over his ears, brushing his shoulders, while his pate was bald.

All of them were wearing black jeans and sleeveless T-shirts, and black combat style boots.

I've no idea why I could recall what they were wearing; I just did. Probably because I was scared.

For the moment, they just stood there, doing nothing. Just staring at us.

Everything seemed to slow down and quieten, as though someone had pressed the mute button on the TV's remote control. Suddenly the leader moved away from the car, sauntering towards us. The other guys followed, lining up alongside him.

Steve first, then one at a time, giving the person in front the time to get out of the van, we stood, glaring back at them as they closed the gap.

You should have seen the look on the men's faces.

A thousand things were going through my mind.

The men stopped mid-stride, looked at us up and down, sizing us up, turned about face, then dashed back to their car with their tails between their legs.

We on the other hand burst out laughing at the sight.

Suddenly I realised things could have turned out worse.

It was hilarious at the time.

We were all scared of what they could have done. I couldn't imagine what it looked like if anyone had driven past.

In fact, it was a comic and a worrying scene. Five old men, against four young men. Doesn't bear thinking about.

As I was writing the whole thing down, I wondered what we would have done if they'd confronted us, especially with Nigel's blood pressure.

Anyhow, it all turned out all right in the end. In spite of all that, it was an unsettling feeling.

And where were the police when you wanted them?

Once we had calmed down and the adrenalin rush had passed, we took off towards Calais and home, as fast as humanly possible. There wasn't a moment to lose, just in case the men decided to try again further down the motorway.

Lady luck must have been looking down on us, as the rest of the journey passed without any more terrifying incidents.

It had been a shock to the system for us all, as it could have turned nasty.

Luckily it didn't, as I was glad, we were on our way home.

We all agreed that we wouldn't mention it to our wives when we next spoke to them, and to wait until we got back to our respective homes, as we didn't want to worry them.

While everything that had just happened was clear in my mind, I pulled the logbook out, writing everything down as quickly as possible as I didn't want to miss anything out. It took me few minutes because my hand was shaking.

Can you credit it, the roads had become busier? Even a couple of police cars passed us.

The next few hours passed without incident. Well, technically speaking, without incident – there were several moments when we slowed down after seeing a car in the distance, similar to the one that had been trying to carjack us. Thankfully, none of them were.

Then it had started to rain, and I wondered if the men would have attempted to stop us if it had been raining. I put that thought to the back of my mind.

We did though, stop at the same service station we stopped on the way down, to grab a bite to eat and to gather our thoughts. Also, the ferry wasn't until 8.25 in the morning, so we had plenty of time, barring any more frightening encounters on the way.

It's not every day you are being forced to stop on a motorway in broad daylight, then subjected by four men, trying to either carjack the motorhome, or steal our possessions.

We only stayed at the service station until we were all in the right frame of mind to carry on.

Just after midnight, we made our way back onto the motorway, then onwards to Calais, the patter of rain on the roof of the van becoming louder, almost violent.

Large raindrops clung to the window, snaking down in crooked rivulets, the windscreen wipers working overtime.

By the time the dawn was casting its light through the morning mist on the Saturday morning, the bright lights of the port and town of Calais slowly came into view.

And it had finally stopped raining.

As we neared the port, we were shocked to see the hundreds of asylum seekers in one of many encampments dotted around the area, rather than anything to do with being, or going on holiday, waiting for their ferry.

There must have been hundreds of blue make-shift tents.

I noticed that there were a few families.

Mostly there was an abundance of men in their twenties who looked a little roughshod and desperate.

They were hanging about in small groups, smoking, and talking in hushed tones, their dishevelled hair and stained clothes adding to the tension as we drove past.

I knew there was still a problem with asylum seekers. I thought the authorities had reduced the numbers. Seems as though I was wrong.

I know it was early, yet I was surprised with the lack of vehicles waiting to board the ferry, especially at this time of year.

On reflection, I would have thought by now, that the vast majority of holidaymakers were getting fed up of waiting for hours to fly abroad, deciding it would be less hassle staying in the UK. Mind you, the average cost for filling the car before we left was £100.

There were also talks of a three-day rail strike this month.

Chapter Thirty-Six

Two hours later, three men in high-vis jackets instructed the lines of vehicles, of every shape and size, to make their way onto the ferry.

With there only being a few vehicles, we were soon parked up, and on our way to one of the decks that had comfy seats, so we could take it easy, hopefully grabbing some shut-eye.

While the others sprawled out on the seats, I made my way to the duty-free to buy some cigarettes I'd promised June.

To be honest, they weren't all that cheap. At least there was a small saving.

I then checked out the books that were on sale, hoping there may have a couple of new ones I hadn't read. No, nothing, so I headed back to the others, hoping to sleep for an hour.

It was Steve who woke me up, telling me we were close to Dover, and if I had any Euro's I wanted changing, it would be best doing it straight away as the bureau de change was closing in ten minutes.

Minutes later we were all gazing over the sea, looking out for the first signs of land. Then in the distant haze over the water, I could see the white cliffs of Dover in all their majesty.

Was there anything so beautiful in the world to an Englishman?

Above the cliffs, white birds soared, welcoming travellers over the channel.

An hour later we were back on British soil.

We followed the snaking cars and vans towards passport control. This time the border control didn't stop and search us as last time, and we were soon heading for home.

We used the time, phoning home, letting them know we were in the UK, driving up the motorway.

Barring any set-backs or hold-ups, we should arrive back around 3 o'clock in the afternoon.

Seeing that the others had done most of the driving in France and Spain, I took the wheel from leaving the M25 all the way to Bradford, finally arriving outside Geoff's house just after at 3 o'clock in the afternoon.

We were shattered.

This time, along with our wives, there was bunting all over the trees in the house opposite and a banner made from a bedsheet, with WELCOME HOME YOU OLD GITS written crudely in black ink hanging from Geoff's bedroom window that faced the road.

It was good to be home.

Our wives and friends crowded round us, asking all sorts of questions, which in an odd kind of way gave me a moment to reflect, stepping back for a moment to think about what we'd achieved, what we'd seen, along with some of the frightening experiences that we'd recently encountered.

After all the hugs and kisses, we spent just an hour talking before we emptied the van of our dirty clothes and other personal belongings. Steve still had a long journey ahead of him to Scotland. We had a two hour drive ourselves. Before we went our separate ways, I said that I would try and turn the logbook into a book.

June drove us home, and it was kind of weird being a passenger in a car rather than a vehicle the size of a garden shed.

As we motored on the M62 towards Liverpool, I thought it best if I didn't tell June about the attempted carjacking, leaving her to read about it in the book.

I slept most of Sunday and into Monday.

June's a volunteer at a charity shop in the local village, so that left me to have an undisturbed sleep on Monday.

To be honest, I was pleased to be getting home, after being in a foreign country for two weeks, then realising that you're absolutely shattered from spending the past two weeks in a constant state of pretending to relax.

Then over the next day or so, trying to recreate eating at the tapas bars in Spain by pulling up a stool in Gregg's.

Recapturing that carefree Mediterranean vibe by having a microwaved ready-meal paella. And 'welcome back, you look well from your wife!' Translation: You're all shiny and appear to have doubled in size.

When you mention to your family and friends that it rained, only for them to say, 'Oh dear, it's been glorious here while you've been away'.

Then the five minutes between exclaiming how brilliant it is to be watching 'normal' telly again, then ten minutes later shouting about how much you hate what's on the telly.

Spending the next year with a Euro in your wallet which you'll keep thinking is a fiver when you desperately need one.

Being able to enter the kitchen without having to do battle with a gigantic double-bodied killer wasp-like beast from Hell.

Managing to completely lose your tan in the first week back home.

Finally, 'can you believe it guys, this time last week we were in . . .

So, that's it really. The story of how four of my best friends in the world and I, ventured on a holiday in the twilight of our years, giving us all life-long memories to look back on.

We had fulfilled what we had set out to do.

The one's on medication took their prescriptions and Nigel's fluctuating blood pressure didn't give him any cause for concern.

Plus the fuel consumption was as we expected, and luckily, we didn't need the spare tyres.

When I was writing this book, I told several people what it was about. Practically all of them said it would be full of stories about five old guys getting pissed in Spain every night. Now that you have finally reached this point in the book, I hope you can agree with me, that was further from the truth.

I do hope you enjoyed reading – Five Old *'Gits'* and a Motorhome.

Like many novels, the story, as mentioned at the beginning of the book, emerged from a number of bizarre incidents that happened to me and my family over a period of time, plus my overworked imagination. That's the beauty of fiction!

When I set about out writing this novel, I wanted the reader to feel by the end of the book that we had gone on holiday. I hope you felt that.

After mentioning earlier on in the book about people going on holiday by ferry instead of being held up at the airports; while I was putting the final touches to the book, there has been massive queues at the ports of Dover and Folkstone as holidaymakers and lorry drivers tried to get to France. The UK government were blaming the delays on the French authorities due to additional checking and stamping of British passports.

Since leaving Brexit, UK citizens no longer have automatic right to move freely within the European Union, therefore the French officials have now to stamp passports and carry out a number of checks including, can you believe it? Asking whether the traveller(s) has enough money to stay ...

Come on ... it's the start of the school holidays and it's the French. What do you expect?

Note from the author

After 'Morocco or bust August '69' was published in 2019, there were two kinds of reviews and messages I often got: the person who said, 'I'd love to do something like that someday' and the ones who said, 'I wish I had done that when I was younger'.

There is no difference between these people – the second is just older than the first and their dreams turned into regret because they had to put it on hold, hoping 'someday' they would find the courage to do it. For them, it was too late.

It isn't too late. If you want excitement and living the dream, go for it.

The one thing I learnt in life when I was younger is that things evolve in ways that you can never plan for, or even predict.

To not do something just because the end result is not in sight is no good reason for not doing it.

The seven of us back in 1969 didn't have a clue what was going to happen to us, or even get back home in one piece.

Now you have everything at your fingertips, so if you want to travel abroad with your mates in a motorhome, or similar, rather than an overpriced package holiday with dozens of screaming children around you, go for it. You won't regret it.

We did, and we didn't regret a moment.

While we were away on holiday in the motorhome it was nothing like a normal holiday where you go from one place to another, checking in at hotels on the way to your final destination, sticking very much to the travel-grid. We didn't fully use the motorhome as we should have.

All we wanted it for, was comfort and to be able to go on holiday together.

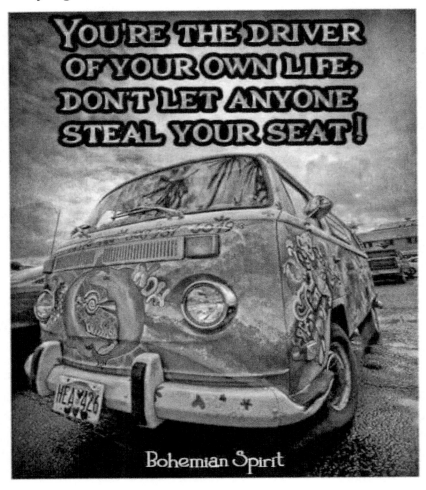

Bohemian Spirit

I can now well imagine, travelling around in a motorhome, giving you access to everywhere, allowing you to see places you probably wouldn't have seen otherwise.

Experiencing all the things in between, plus you get a taste of the whole country you're visiting. Going on holiday in a van will give you views that no one else can even get and a view that would cost you a great deal of money if you had been staying in hotels.

As far as I was concerned, there was nothing better than waking up in a beautiful place and stepping outside to watch the sunrise with a cup of coffee.

My goodness I miss those days . . .

A generation that walked to school and then walked back home

A generation that did their homework alone to get out asap to play in the street

A generation that spent all their free time on the street with their friends

A generation that played hide and seek when dark

A generation that made mud cakes

A generation that collected sports cards

A generation that found, collected, and washed & returned empty pop bottles to the local grocery store for a few pence, then bought another bottle of pop and a bar of chocolate with the money

A generation that made paper toys with their bare hands

A generation who bought vinyl albums to play on record players

A generation that collected photos and albums of clippings

A generation that played board games and cards on rainy days

A generation whose TV went off at midnight after playing the National Anthem

A generation that had parents who were there

A generation that laughed under the covers in bed, so parents didn't know we were still awake

A generation that is passing and unfortunately it will never return

I LOVED growing up when I did

"Age is an issue of mind over matter. If you don't mind, it doesn't matter." ~*Mark Twain*

"Funny thing about getting older: Your eyesight starts getting weaker but your ability to see through people's bullshit gets much better." ~*Morgan Freeman.*

***

In 1969 they said they went to the moon (or did they?) You saw them playing golf and driving a moon buggy, and talking to Nixon from a landline telephone, 238,000 miles away – 0 second delay.

Yet in 2017, on the ISS, 294 miles away – 11 second delay.

One step for man, one giant step for mankind. Unfortunately, we cannot go back because we destroyed that technology from 1969.

We've been told that it's a very painful process to build it back again . . . YET, we can go to Mars, which is 200 times further than the moon.

I will leave that with you to digest.

Over the past 50+ years, we've witnessed some of the most profound changes in human history.

Between a pandemic, wars, technological developments, progress in civil rights, breakthroughs in science and medicine.

The old order has been swept away, sometimes giving way to freer forms of governing and sometimes not.

Centuries-old empires crumbled as new ideologies – from communism to fascism – took root in many parts of the world.

Wars in the early part of the 20th century led to the end of the colonial world, giving birth to new nations.

Throughout the past century, technological innovations transformed our lives in ways we never dreamed of.

Progressive ideas also emerged that changed the world as women, African Americans, and the LGBTQ community demanded, and often won, equal rights – from the ratification of the 19th Amendment in the United States to the legalization of same-sex marriage in many countries around the world.

Even so, recent civil rights protests tell us the fight for equality is not over.

Personal home computers began to emerge in the 1970s, yet many of the earliest versions resembled calculators that would plug into televisions sets. By 1977, however, the desktop home computer begins to resemble their more modern versions – with an accompanying attached or separate computer screen and a magnetic tape or floppy disk storage device.

The Commodore PET is unveiled at the Consumer Electronics Show in Chicago that year, while the first Apple II and Radio Shack's TRS-80 go on sale.

The internet as we know it today is born in 1983 – a seemingly endless collection of websites hosted on servers scattered across the globe – is still more than a decade away. At the beginning of 1983, the Advanced Research Projects Agency Network (ARPANET) – a small network for academics and researchers – transitions to the standard TCP/IP protocol of the World Wide Web. The protocol would become the internet's cornerstone and technical foundation as it allows expanded available address space and decentralizes the network, thus also expanding accessibility.

In 1984, Amazon.com is born, with an initial aim of becoming an online bookstore. Jeff Bezos and a handful of angel investors launch Amazon.com, just as e-commerce is about to take off.

In 2020, after expanding from books to the so-called "Everything Store," growing a business, selling cloud services to companies like Netflix and Instagram, Bezos would be the world's richest man.

1998, the age of Google begins, with seed money from Sun Microsystems co-founder Andy Bechtolsheim and Amazon founder Jeff Bezos, among others, Stanford University Ph.D.

students Larry Page and Sergey Brin launch the search engine Google.

The digital advertising behemoth Google Inc., now Alphabet Inc., is a $1.104 trillion company with several subsidiaries, including video-sharing platform YouTube; autonomous-car development company Waymo; and X, the company's research, and development division.

2004, Facebook was founded. Mark Zuckerberg, a 23-year-old Harvard University student, creates "The Facebook," a local social networking site named after the orientation materials that profiles students and faculty, giving to incoming college freshmen. Sixteen years later, Facebook has become an $843.6 billion digital advertising behemoth so integral to many people's lives that it has been criticized for helping foreign powers and propagandists influence the U.S. political system.

2007, the iPhone is available. Apple CEO, Steve Jobs, who died in October 2011, first showed the world one of the most popular branded consumer electronic devices in history, the iPhone.

Since the first generation phone that Jobs introduced at the Consumer Electronics Show that year, there have been 18 versions of the mobile device. More than 1.2 billion units have been sold globally through 2017. Only Samsung's Galaxy smartphone comes close to that volume. All said and done, why has it taken this long to get where we are now?

There's nothing on the Earth that hasn't been here for hundreds of thousands of years.

Could it be alien technology?

That's a story for another day . . .

Finally, the Covid-19 pandemic that was ravaging the world in 2020/2021 reminds us that for all of our scientific breakthroughs, we're still vulnerable to deadly viruses that can shut down economies and disrupt society. The virus spread to Europe and the United States in early 2020 and was declared a pandemic by the World Health Organization on March 11.

The outbreak reached virtually every nation on Earth, leading to countrywide lockdowns, massive layoffs, business closures, and school shutdowns.

You may think

that you are completely insignificant in this world. But someone drinks coffee from the favourite cup you gave them.

Someone heard a song on the radio that reminded them of you.

Someone read the book that you recommended and plunged headfirst into it.

Someone smiled after a hard day's work because they remembered the joke that you told them.

Someone loves themselves a little bit more because you gave them a compliment.

Never think that you have no influence on people's lives whatsoever.

Your trace, which you leave behind with every good deed, cannot be erased.

UNKNOWN

Once upon a time! When Window was just a square hole in a room and Application was something written on paper. When Keyboard was a Piano and Mouse just an animal. When File was an important office material and Hard Drive just an uncomfortable road trip. When Cut was done with a knife and Paste with glue. When Web was a spider's home and Virus was flu. When Junk Mail were printed flyers posted through your letterbox. When Apple and Blackberry were just fruits – that's when we had a lot of time for family and friends.

Get Back !

Let's go back to the Sixties

When we were spoilt for choice,

Remember all those pop groups

And the singers with a voice...

The Fifties passed us Rock N Roll

And this we carried on,

But in the wink of an eye, you'd see some cry

When Buddy Holly was gone....

So, then it was the Mersey Sound

A Revolution we were havin',

Made famous by the Fab Four

Who were playing it in the Cavern

We didn't have computers,

No sign of Mobile Phones,

But we could listen to Rhythm and Blues

Played by the Rolling Stones...

Folk Music from the Seekers

And Jazz from Kenny Ball

Progressive Music from The Cream

The radio played them all...

But don't forget the Geordie Groups

They all had their own sounds

Eric Burdon and the Animals

With Alan Price were doing the rounds. . .

Mini Skirts and Mini Car

Beer at one and ten a Jar,

Rockets we saw reach the moon

(Don't think we're going there too soon) . . ..

Tamla Motown played out loud

Always stood out from the crowd

Whatever happened to Motor City ?

Not here now and more's the pity. . .

Country Music sounding Fine,

Johnny Cash and Patsy Cline

Easy listening, never a hurry

Hearing songs from Anne Murray. . .

Well, you may think Sixties gone

But I can tell you, you'd be wrong,

How come ? I here you asking, Why ?

Well, it's there on YouTube and Spotify !!!

© Chalkey (Geoff S) 2021

***

A bit of nostalgia

REMEMBER WHEN:-

It took five minutes for the TV to warm up

Nearly everyone's Mum was home when the kids got home from school.

Nobody owned a purebred dog.

You'd reach into a muddy gutter for a penny.

Your Mother wore nylons that came in two pieces.

All male teachers wore ties and female teachers had their hair done every day and wore high heels.

You got your windscreen cleaned, oil checked, and petrol served, without asking, all for free, every time...

It was considered a great privilege to be taken out to dinner at a real restaurant with your parents.

They threatened to keep children back a year if they failed the school year... And they did!

When a Ford Zephyr was everyone's dream car...and people went steady.

Spinning around, getting dizzy and falling down was cause for giggles?

Playing cricket with no adults to help the children with the rules of the game.

Bottles came from the corner shop without safety caps and hermetic seals because no one had yet tried to poison a perfect stranger.

And with all our progress, don't you wish, just once, you could slip back in time and savour the slower pace, and share it with the children of today?

When being sent to the headmasters office was nothing compared to the fate that awaited you at home.

Basically, we were in fear for our lives, but it wasn't because of drive-by shootings, drugs, gangs etc.

Our parents and grandparents were a much bigger threat! But we survived because their love was greater than the threat.

As well as summers filled with bike rides, cricket, Hula Hoops, skating and visits to the pool, eating lemonade powder or liquorice sticks.

Didn't that feel good, just to go back and say, 'Yes, I remember that'?

Who can remember that the perfect age is somewhere between old enough to know better and too young to care?

Who can still remember the Lone Ranger and Sgt Bilko?

Coca Cola in bottles.

Blackjacks and bubble gums.

Home milk delivery in glass bottles with tinfoil tops.

Hi-fi's & 45 RPM records.

78 RPM records!

Adding Machines.

Scalextric.

Do You Remember a Time When. . .?

Decisions were made by going 'Eeny-meeny-miney-moe'?

'Race issue' meant arguing about who ran the fastest?

Catching tadpoles could happily occupy an entire day?

It wasn't odd to have two or three 'Best Friends'?

The worst thing you could catch from the opposite sex was 'chickenpox'?

Having a Weapon in School meant being caught with a Catapult ?

(we used to unwind the core of Golf balls for the elastic!)

War was a card game? according to Hoyle!

Cigarette cards in the spokes transformed any bike into a motorcycle.

Taking drugs meant orange - flavoured chewable aspirin.

Water balloons were the ultimate weapon.

If you can remember most or all of these, Then you have LIVED!!

(Margaret Mcintosh 2022)

Morocco Or Bust, August '69: A True Story

https://www.amazon.co.uk/Morocco-Bust-August-Michael-Rowland-ebook/dp/B07QPNHK8M/ref=sr_1_fkmr0_2?crid=19A43NBDP5CQI&keywords=michael+rowland+9%2F11&qid=1658925991&sprefix=Michael+rowland+9%2F11%2Caps%2C64&sr=8-2-fkmr0

2017/05/04

Remember – good friends are the rare jewels in life, difficult to
find and impossible to replace.

***

Your old life can seem like some strange distant dream, like it
might never have even existed, and before you know it, decades
have passed you by. And it's only family and close friends you
are with who will fully understand. They are the ones who
know what's going on.

Printed in Great Britain
by Amazon

84344400R10149